Hell in Paradise Valley

Barry Cord

G.K. Hall & Co. • **Thorndike, Maine**

Published in 1999 by arrangement with Golden West Literary Agency.

Barry Cord is a pseudonym of Peter B. Germano.

G.K. Hall Large Print Paperback Series.

The text of this Large Print edition is unabridged.
Other aspects of the book may vary from the original edition.

Set in 16 pt. Plantin.

Printed in the United States on permanent paper.

Library of Congress Cataloging-in-Publication Data

Cord, Barry, 1913–
    Hell in Paradise Valley / Barry Cord.
       p.   cm.
       ISBN 0-7838-8739-6 (lg. print : sc : alk. paper)
       1. Large type books. I. Title.
    [PS3505.O6646H45   1999]
    813′.54—dc21   99-36807

Also by Barry Cord
in Large Print:

Last Chance at Devil's Canyon

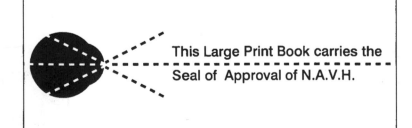

This Large Print Book carries the
Seal of Approval of N.A.V.H.

Hell in
Paradise Valley

I

Dave Owens sat cross-legged, an old carbine across his lap, staring through the thin screen of buckbrush down the long, gently rolling valley that showed no signs of life. He had been here before sunup, waiting. Now the sun was high, burning a hole in the gunmetal sky, searing the ground below.

A dozen trail herds had come this way, out of Texas. The deep trace of their passage had churned this valley floor to dust, prey now to any vagrant wind.

It had not rained since March and the winter preceding had been one of the driest on record. Now in late August, the low hills flanking the valley were like tinderboxes. A careless cigarette and a rising wind could start a conflagration among the brush on the slopes that would burn unchecked for miles.

The sweat rolled down Dave's cheeks, hesitated at the chin line, then fell drop by drop on the hard, dry ground. A gnat buzzed past his face and came back, attracted by the salt sweat on his upper lip. He brushed it away.

Behind him a small canyon pierced the hills, dying a quarter of a mile within. At the mouth of the canyon, and some fifty yards from where he waited, a brackish-looking pool fed by underground springs attracted a swarm of gnats which buzzed in a mad dance low over the surface. Yielding to the burning sun, the water had receded slowly from its normal mark, leaving a twenty-foot stretch of dry, wattled mud in testimony of its defeat.

Dave let his gaze stray to the water hole. His canteen was empty, his mouth parched. His body was crying for moisture, but he made no move toward the water that lay just below him.

He pulled his gaze away from the pool and fixed it on a distant point downvalley.

They should be showing up about now, he thought . . . they have to show up!

He was gambling his life on it.

II

Jess Riley turned in his saddle to look back down the long hot valley where eighteen hundred mixed Texas cattle, all road branded Circle T, were strung out, moving slowly toward him. The flank riders were busy driving back lean-bellied steers foraging in draws and gullies. The drag men were hidden in the dust and heat-hazed disturbance.

Every man riding for him was putting in a twenty-four hour day, and Jess knew they were bone weary and edgy.

The trail boss felt the sour taste of anger rise in his throat. He had five hundred head of his own in that strung-out herd and he knew at this point he'd be lucky to break even.

Drought had forced him and his west Texas neighbors, all small ranchers, to pool their beef in a drive north, although it was late in the season and Jess knew he'd be driving to a glutted market and tumbling prices. But it was a chance they had to take, or watch their cattle starve. Eyeing those tired, thirsty cattle move up the valley toward him, Jess felt the weight of his responsibility. He had to get this herd to market or he and his friends faced disaster.

He shifted his attention to the rolling hills ahead. Walnut Creek was still a hard day's drive away and his cattle hadn't had water in two days.

Bad luck goes with the last herd up the Trail, was an old Texas saying; it had proven true for Jess. They had lost a hundred head in a freak cloudburst that had poured water into the Brazos and left the surrounding country bone dry. It should have been an omen.

Accident and sickness had taken their toll of his drovers thereafter, and by the time they reached Indian Tanks Jess was shorthanded and pressed for time. From where he stood he knew it was a fifty-fifty chance he'd lose half that herd before he reached his destination.

But Jess was a stubborn man. He stood a bit over six feet tall in his boots, wide across the shoulders, with a rider's lean flanks and quick reflexes. His hair was brown, but Texas suns had streaked it light. His eyes were gray and direct, his mouth hard. He was nudging thirty: a man

9

who knew his own mind, and was his own man.

He turned his gaze to a distant patch of green that seemed to lay against the low, bare hills. There was water there and just thinking about it made him thirsty. He reached down for his canteen — then remembered he had not filled up this morning. Everyone was on short water rations.

A rider popped out of a gully several hundred yards away, saw Jess and spurred toward him.

Randy Williams was young, wiry, reckless. His straw hair should have been red, to match his temper. He was always on a short fuse, but he calmed down quickly, and his saving grace was that he apologized when he was wrong, which was often enough.

Randy had been up the trail with Jess before, and if he made any effort to control his temper it was with the trail boss.

He pulled up alongside Jess and rubbed the back of his hand across his lips.

"Got any water left?"

The trail boss shook his head.

"Mouth's like cotton," Randy growled. He glanced up the long valley. "Gonna be a long dry ride to Walnut Creek."

Jess pointed. "Might still be some water left in Box Springs."

Randy stood up in his stirrups, looking ahead. "Hell — what are we waiting for?" He settled back and dug in his spurs, his horse leaping away from Jess's.

They raced toward the spring. Halfway there Randy's horse stumbled, then began to limp. Jess went past the younger man as Randy dismounted to check the animal.

"Hey!" Randy yelled. "Save some for me."

Jess settled into an easy jog. His mouth seemed to get drier the closer he got to the water hole.

He dismounted twenty yards from the glint of water and went forward slowly, testing the firmness of the wattled mud rimming the Springs. Sunlight sparkled on the still surface; in the shade, gnats buzzed just above the water line.

Jess headed for the shady area, knowing that the brackish water would be cooler there. He was down on his hands and knees, about to bury his face into it when a bullet created a small geyser about a foot from his head. The crack of the carbine had been instantaneous, indicating the rifleman was close by.

Jess jerked back, his hand streaking for his holstered gun.

Dave's voice was quick, hoarse. "Hold it, mister!" He moved into view on the slope above him. He was shorter than the Texas trail boss, and about Randy's age. A stubble of dark beard around his mouth and jaw made him look older.

"That water's poisoned!" he added harshly.

He started to walk down to Jess, his rifle hanging loosely at his side. "I didn't see you right away . . . then it was too late to yell out."

Behind Jess his roan began to move toward the

water, dragging his reins.

"Better keep him away," Dave added quickly. "I almost lost mine."

Jess grabbed the roan's bit and held the animal back. His mouth was parched — and the water was tantalizingly near, innocently inviting.

He eyed the oncoming man. "You sure?"

Dave came up and took hold of Jess's bridle. Go ahead," he suggested. "Check it yourself."

Jess hesitated. Dave smiled tightly and handed the trail boss his carbine. He wasn't wearing a hand gun.

"You smelled strychnine before?"

Jess nodded. He went to the water's edge, crouched and brought a handful up to his face. He straightened, wiping his hands on his pants.

"There's an empty can of the stuff out there in the brush," Dave said. He waved across the water hole. "Found it just as I was leaving."

They both turned as Randy came riding up on a limping horse. The young rider had a gun in his hand.

Jess made a quick motion. "No trouble, Randy! Put that gun away!"

Randy studied the stranger for a moment before holstering his Colt.

"Looks like we stay dry until we hit the river," Jess growled. He motioned to the water. "Strychnine."

Randy swore.

Jess turned to the man holding his horse; he handed Dave his carbine. "I'm Jess Riley," he

12

said. "That's Randy Williams, my *segundo*."

The other nodded. "Heard about you. I'm Dave Owens." He paused for a moment, his glance going to Randy who was studying him. "I've got a small herd coming up behind yours. About a day's ride back."

Jess frowned. "Thought we were the last ones up the trail."

Dave shrugged.

Randy tied his horse to a sapling and walked to the water's edge. He dipped his hand into it, tasted it . . . and made a wry, angry face.

Dave said harshly, "Can't understand why anyone would want to poison a water hole way out here!"

"Some goddamn farmer!" Randy snapped. "We've been having trouble with them since we left Indian Tanks."

He eyed Dave as he walked back to his horse. "They been leaving you alone?"

"So far."

Dave turned to the trail boss. "I started out shorthanded, got as far as the Tanks. Lost one man in a freak accident; the other ran out of whiskey and quit. There's just me and my wife now . . . and an old Mexican. I rode up ahead to hire some help." He shook his head, his eyes hard, bitter. "You'd think I was some horse thief, the way some of these ranchers acted."

"I know what you mean," Jess growled.

He turned to Randy. "Get back to the herd. Tell the boys to keep them away from here." He

13

glanced up at the sun. "We won't be bedding down tonight. Turn that mare of yours in for something that'll carry you 'til we hit the river. Pass the word to the others."

Dave watched Randy ride off. He turned to the trail boss and said, "Hope you have better luck than I've been having."

"Thanks," Jess said shortly. "Sorry I can't help, but I'm shorthanded myself."

Dave nodded. "I understand."

He started to walk away.

Jess felt uncomfortable. Damn it, the man had probably saved his life. He was likeable — and they shared a common plight.

He said, "Hey, wait a minute."

Dave turned.

"How far back you say your herd was?"

"Just the other side of Indian Tanks."

Jess considered. He was less than five days' drive from his destination, and he could use an extra hand. . . .

"How about your wife? She all right?"

Dave smiled. "I told her I might be gone some time. And the old Mex keeps an eye on things. There's enough graze and water where we're camped."

"Enough to hold them a week or so?"

"I wouldn't want to be away longer," Dave said. "But I think they could hold out all right."

The trail boss made up his mind then. "You give me a hand with my herd and I'll help you get yours up the trail."

Dave hesitated. "I need more than one hand. . . ."

"I think I can talk some of my boys into helping out," Jess cut in. He held out his hand. "Is it a deal?"

Dave glanced off, hiding the small gleam of satisfaction in his eyes. Then he turned and took Jess's hand.

"It's a deal," he said.

III

Hank Larabee, chuck-wagon cook and hard-nosed tyrant, eyed the man who rode up with Jess with a speculative, cynical glance. He had lost his galley slave and wood-gatherer, a pimply faced homesick boy who had claimed an attack of worms as a face-saving gesture, just after crossing the Canadian.

Like Randy, Hank had come up the trail with Jess before. He was part of the nucleus of old hands, like Chuck Wallis, Larry Overton and Bob Rich. By this time he knew the trail from Arroyo Grande where they had started in Texas to Kansas like he knew his chuck wagon. He had started out as a farmer, until his wife died in childbirth — when he had attached himself to Jess as handyman and cook on Jess's bachelor spread. Now he went where Jess went.

The trail boss's introduction was short and to the point. "Dave Owens. He's got a small herd stalled on the trail behind us. Hell give you a hand."

"We camping at the Springs?"

Jess shook his head. "Someone poisoned the water hole."

Hank cursed. "Just one goddamn thing after another, this trip . . ."

Jess cut him off. "We're pushing on through to the river. Make camp up by the bluffs. 'Round about midnight some of the boys will come in — give them some chow and an hour's sleep, then move on up to the river."

Hank nodded.

Jess gave Dave a small smile and rode off.

Hank eyed the new hand. "I'm Mister Larabee," he said coldly. "My job is to keep ten hungry men fed so they can keep riding sixteen hours a day an' not come down with worms, jaundice or boils. I get a four-horse team to look after, axle wheels to keep greased, water barrels to keep filled an' sugar thieves out of my staples. I can't make hot biscuits without a fire — that'll be just one of your jobs. I want anything that'll burn. That won't be easy to find, seeing as how a dozen other herds have come up this trail before us." He paused. "That understood, Mr. Owens?"

Owens took his hat off and ran fingers through his damp, curly hair. "Sounds fair enough. When do I start?"

"Right now. Help me grease this wheel. We've got to beat them to the bluffs — that's about ten miles from here. We set up temporary camp, get a fire going. The boys'll be straggling in all hours of the night an' they'll be hungry an' testy. We feed them, take their sass, let them get forty winks an' head them back to the herd."

Dave grinned. "When do we sleep?"

Hank's faded blue eyes turned cold. "When we get those cows all bedded down at the river."

Dave dismounted, tying his horse to the wagon tailgate. He looked downvalley to where the herd was moving in a small cloud of dust. His mouth was dry.

He said, "I could use a drop of water."

Hank motioned to the water barrel strapped to the side of the wagon. "Help yourself."

Dave picked up the tin cup fastened to the side of the barrel by a small leather thong, turned the spigot and let a little water fall in. He moistened his cracked lips first, then swallowed.

Hank said in a kindlier tone, "I see the boss told you we're short on water."

Dave nodded and finished what was left.

They took the left rear wheel off and greased it. The herd had gone by them when they finished.

Hank said, "You work pretty good." He said it in a sort of grudging tone; for he was used to hands who groused at having to do anything around the chuck wagon.

Dave untied his horse. "Need anything else done?" His smile was quick and easy and Hank responded to it.

"Not until we make camp at the bluffs."

Dave mounted. Hank looked up at him. "Mr. Riley said you have a herd of your own . . . ?"

Dave nodded. "Not as big as this." He turned his head and glanced upvalley. "How far to King City?"

"Four days' drive — after we make Walnut Creek." Hank frowned slightly. "Your first drive up the trail?"

Dave grinned. "It shows?"

"Has to be a first time for everybody." Hank smiled. He did not usually smile, but he was warming to this new hand.

"This part's the worst of it," Hank added. "Be easier after we cross the river."

He climbed up onto the wagon seat. "See what you can find for firewood."

Dave waved and rode off.

Hank watched him for a moment, trying to understand the small nagging behind his thoughts. He liked Dave first off, which was unusual for the forty-seven year old man the younger men called "Pop", which he resented. Still, there was something behind Dave's smiling, ready-to-please front that didn't fit: something hard and ruthless and selfish.

"Aw, leave the boy alone!" he chided himself.

He picked up his reins and headed for the bluffs.

Most of the herd was well past the poisoned water hole by late afternoon, moving northeast in a cloud of dust.

Randy Williams, mounted on a fresh horse, looked down at the yearling down on its side a few yards away. The animal was dying.

Randy whirled to face the man astride the saddle next to him. "Dammit, Lin! I told you to keep them away from this water!"

Lin Waters, a slat-thin, round-shouldered man who had seen better and younger days, reacted to Randy's harshness. His pale gray eyes flashed angrily above his ragged brown mustache.

"I can't cover the whole flank, Randy!"

"Just your part will be enough!" Randy snapped.

Waters stiffened, his face turning pale and tight. His hand slid down to his holstered gun, driven there by the contempt in Randy's voice . . . then he turned slightly as Jess Riley rode up.

"What's wrong?"

Randy flashed a hand to the dying steer.

"I tried to head her off," Lin said in a thin, strained voice. "But I can't be everywhere." He saw Randy sneer and he said bitterly, "I've worked my tail off on this trip, Mr. Riley. But if you don't like the way I'm doing my job, pay me off right now . . ."

"Might not be a bad idea," Randy cut in.

Jess said coldly, "Shut up, Randy!"

Randy settled back in his saddle, his eyes narrowed and hurt. "Maybe you'd rather pay *me* off, Jess?"

"If it comes to that, yes!" Jess said evenly. He looked into Randy's eyes and added, before the younger man embarked on a decision he could not back down from: "We got a tired, hungry, thirsty herd to get to the river before half of them die on us. I'm not letting anybody quit on me!"

He turned to the older man. "Hank's headed for the river. Go give him a hand. Tell that new man, Dave, I want him to spell Larry on drag."

Lin flushed, knowing he was being let off the hook. Pride forced him to say what was really unnecessary. "I do my job, Mr. Riley."

Jess nodded. "*I'll* tell you when you're not, Lin!"

He waited until the man had gone before turning to Randy.

"He was dogging it!" His segundo snarled. "He had plenty of time to cut that yearling back."

"Worn out, maybe," Jess contradicted. "Anyway, we can't afford to lose any more men."

Randy eyed the water hole. From somewhere, and the Lord knows, he thought, a turkey buzzard had sensed death and was even now settling on a gnarled dead branch less than fifty yards away. It would wait there until they rode away. Randy stifled an impulse to draw and shoot the ugly carrion eater. Letting his gaze fall on the sparkling water instead, he was immediately conscious of his dry, cottony mouth.

"Got any water?" he growled.

Jess handed him his canteen. He had half filled it at the chuck wagon.

Randy allowed himself two swallows, wiped his lips with the back of his hand and sighed.

"Well be all right once we hit the river," Jess said. He glanced off, his eyes hard. "We've got them moving in the right direction, but it won't take much to get them turned around. They're half crazed with thirst now."

Randy handed him back his canteen. "Ain't been nothing but trouble this trip. Some of the boys are talking about this drive being Jonahed —"

He paused at something he saw in Jess's face and looked off.

A half-dozen riders were coming toward them, appearing, it seemed, from out of the low, flanking hills. They rode like men not used to saddles, but some of them carried shotguns across their pommels.

Randy said angrily, "Another non-welcoming committee!" and slid his hand to his gun-butt.

The group pulled up a few feet away, sullen and angrily fearful. All of them wore bib overalls; none of them looked prosperous. The older men were stooped and weathered by sun and wind and toil, their faces eroded by long, worrisome years.

Two were boys, not more than fifteen or sixteen. The others were in their forties.

They clustered around a blocky, straw-haired

man with a flat-crowned hat set squarely on his head. They waited for him to speak

He looked at Jess. "You the boss of this trail outfit?"

Jess nodded.

"I'm Mike Cobb," the man said. "My sons," he nodded to the boys, "and neighbors, Matt, Liggett and Bracken. We got farms up the way apiece — just this of Walnut Creek."

Jess waited, saying nothing.

Mike shifted uncomfortably. "We're not here to make trouble for you, mister. We know how it's been with all you Texas drovers . . . it's been a bad year for all of us."

The man called Liggett, a thin, wispy-haired man said uneasily, "Believe us . . . any other year and we'd be happy to see you."

"But not this year, eh?" Randy's voice was cold.

The farmers looked at him. One of Mike's boys slid his thumb lightly over the hammer of his old twenty-gauge shotgun.

Mike said, holding down his anger, "We've had our fences tore down, what feed we been hoarding trampled, our water fouled. That ain't right, is it, mister?"

He was looking at Jess, and the trail boss shook his head. "We'll keep our cows off your land," he promised.

Mike relaxed. "Ain't that we mean to be inhospitable . . ."

"Poisoning a waterhole ain't exactly friendly!"

Randy exploded.

Mike looked blank for a moment, then turned and eyed the dead steer for the first time. His gaze moved on to the water hole, glinting innocently in the dying day.

"We were lucky," Randy added edgily. "We could have lost a couple of men, as well as a lot more cows."

Mike looked at his companions, puzzled. "Don't know who'd do a thing like that. We don't need this water."

"But we do," Randy said. He was staring coldly at them, his hand on his gun.

Jess headed him off. "We're not blaming anybody here." He eased his horse between Randy and the farmers. "I've got eighteen hundred thirsty cows to get to King City. I'm short of hands. If any of you . . ."

Mike said quickly, "Sorry, mister. But we got all the work we can handle." He nodded to the others and they started to turn.

"If I hear of anybody looking for work, I'll tell them you're hiring."

Jess watched them ride back the way they had come. Randy let out an angry breath.

"Someone poisoned that water hole!" he said harshly. "It had to be one of them."

Jess said, "Maybe." But there was a small frown in his eyes as he looked upvalley.

Mike Cobb was right. They didn't need this water. Why bring unnecessary trouble on themselves?

As they rode away, the turkey buzzard flapped down off the limb and settled on the carcass. Before he had torn loose a beakful he was joined by two others, planing in out of the darkening sky.

IV

Dave Owens hawked dust from back in his throat and spat on the ground. He glanced at the rider chousing a steer back from the brush and studied him for a moment, then reached in his back pocket, took out a folded, blue-checkered handkerchief and tied it across the bridge of his nose.

Dave rode into the raised dust, slapping at lagging animals with the trailing short end of his rope, angling toward the rider who, spotting him, started to ride in his direction.

The rider was a lanky man whose cheerfulness showed through the layers of fatigue. He was in his early twenties, blue-eyed, sandy-haired. His hands were rope-scarred. He wore a holster gun on his left hip, butt facing inward for a cross draw. From above the neckerchief that bridged his nose his bright blue eyes took in Dave.

"Hi," he said. His voice was muffled.

Dave said, "You Larry?"

The other nodded.

"I'm Dave Owens. New hand. I'm here to relieve you for a spell."

Larry pulled the neckerchief down from his nose. "Larry Overton." He held out his hand. "Glad to see you." He grinned as they shook. "I need a drink. Where's the next water?"

"The river," Dave said.

"Ain't there a water hole somewhere around here?"

"It's poisoned." Dave shrugged. "Some hot-headed farmer, probably."

"Oh, hell!" Larry sighed. For a moment the bubbling good humor faded from his eyes. Then he shrugged. "Might have expected it. 'Bout everything else has happened on this trip."

A steer lumbered by, tongue lolling. It sank to its knees a few yards away.

Larry rode to him and dismounted. "Come on, you lazy bastard," he said cheerfully. He took hold of the steer's tail and hauled up. "Come on!" he wheedled. "There's a whole river of water ahead. You can lay down there."

The animal staggered to its feet. Larry mounted and slapped at its hind end with his rope. The steer lumbered off to join the others.

"Keep an eye on the muleys," Larry told Dave. "There's a couple of them dogging it."

Dave eyed him. "Muleys?" The question popped out of him, and then his eyes showed he was sorry the moment he said it.

Larry was looking off and didn't see it. But he heard the question. He turned. "Yeah." He pointed to a cow with sprouts of horn showing. It was dropping back, sidling toward a gully,

25

angling back into the hills.

"There's one of them. The other's a black an' white sonuvabitch . . . he's the worse. Let them cut away an' they'll take half the herd with them."

Dave grinned. "I'll keep the sonuvabitches in line." He spurred off, heading the muley back, popping his rope as he had seen Larry do.

Larry watched him for a moment, a frown in his eyes. Then he shrugged, swung his tired animal away, and headed for the wagon which was moving faster than the herd, far up the valley.

They made the river at sunup the next day. The water was low, but flowing: a narrow stream running over a gravel bed. The tired drovers had a job pulling steers out of boggy sand patches and stringing them out along the bank.

It was midmorning when the herd drifted across to the other side and settled. Jess let them wander off in search of forage; he knew they would not wander far. Right now he and his men needed all the rest they could get.

He put two men on the first watch and rotated them every four hours. Dave volunteered for the first trick despite the fatigue showing in every line of his face.

The cattle settled down in the evening. Dave came back and helped Hank with the chores. He seemed determined to please.

They rounded up the herd at dawn and headed them up the trail. The rest had done wonders for the men and the cattle and everyone were in good spirits.

Randy pulled up alongside Jess as the trail boss paused on a small rise flanking the herd.

"That new man, Dave . . . you notice anything funny about him?"

Jess eyed him.

"Works harder than the rest of us," Jess said, "and doesn't complain."

Randy said, "Hell, that ain't what I mean. I'd like him better if he groused a little. But there's something else. . . ."

"What are you getting at?"

Randy looked thoughtful. "For one thing, he doesn't seem to worry too much about leaving his wife alone back there."

Jess shrugged. "You can't always tell what goes on inside a man."

Randy nodded. "I'll go along with that. But for a man who claims to have a herd stalled around Indian Tanks, he doesn't know a hell of a lot about cows. Larry says he doesn't know a muley from a mossback — and he never talks about where he's from."

"Reckon that's his business," Jess replied. "I hired him on to help with this drive, not to find out his personal history. And he's done more than his share."

Randy was silent for a moment.

"You going back to Indian Tanks with him?"

"I gave him my word," Jess said.

"Reckon I'll tag along, too." Randy looked

after the herd moving slowly out of sight. "You talk to any of the boys?"

"Hank likes Dave — he's going. I think Larry, Chuck and Rich will come along. They're young and they don't have anybody waiting for them back home."

Randy knuckled his jaw. "Still can't figger a man who'd go off and leave his wife like that!"

A half-day out of King City, two representatives of the Askins Cattle Company rode out to meet them.

They made a deal on the spot. It was less than Jess had hoped for, but better than he could expect. The long drought had sent grain prices soaring and made it unprofitable to keep trail cattle in holding pens to fatten them up.

Jess took part of the money in cash so he could pay off his hands; the rest was on a bank draft. He did not want to be carrying a lot of cash on him on the long trip back to Texas.

Randy, Larry, Hank, Chuck and Rich confirmed with Jess their intention of riding with him to Indian Tanks. The others had had enough of trailing cattle for this season. But all of them wanted one night in King City before heading back.

Jess had his drink with the boys, then found his way to the barber shop and a warm bath. He had "run the towns" at the end of the trail before, whooped it up, got drunk, put in the calaboose, busted windows, had his fights; he was through with them. Maybe, he thought, he was getting old.

He was having an early breakfast next morning in the hotel restaurant when Dave came in and joined him. Shaved and rested, Jess noticed, Dave was a good-looking man. But he seemed vaguely worried and uneasy as he pulled up a chair and sat across from the trail boss.

He declined Jess's offer of breakfast. He had already eaten, he said. He wanted to say something else, but didn't quite know how to start.

Jess made it easy for him.

"Let's round out the others and start back."

Dave's grin held a great relief. "You know," he said, "I've been feeling a little bad about the whole thing. It's already been a long, hard drive for you. If you want to back out now I could understand."

Jess fixed him with a cold look.

"You don't know me very well, do you?"

Dave moved his shoulders in an apologetic gesture. "Heard about you along the trail. A hard man, they said, but a fair one. And a good man with a gun, if it comes to that."

"And a stubborn one," Jess added airily. "I promised you I'd help you get your herd to wherever you're going with it. If you knew me at all, you'd know my word is good."

"Sorry," Dave said. "I guess I'm just worried about . . . my wife."

"I'd be," Jess said. He rose and put money on the table. They went outside.

It took a half-hour to round up the others and another thirty minutes to get them saddled and ready to ride.

"You planning to drive to King City?" Randy asked. He had tied one on last night and his eyes were half closed to ease the pain behind them.

Dave shook his head. "Place called Paradise Valley."

Jess was surprised. This was the first time he had heard Dave say where he was headed. He should have asked, he thought . . . not that it mattered much.

"I know most of the cattlemen up there," he told Dave. "Some of them are Texans. Came up out of the Panhandle. Hear they're having it rough this year."

"Like all of us," Randy growled. He glanced at Dave. "Why Paradise Valley?"

"Plan to settle there. Bought a small ranch from a man name of Jenkins."

"Old Slip Jenkins?" Jess was surprised again.

"He signed himself George Clayton Jenkins," Dave said levelly.

Jess laughed. "Never knew him by anything but Slip. Never was a friendly sort, either."

Randy leaned forward in the saddle. "Paradise Valley ain't more than seventy miles from Indian Tanks. Why didn't you ride up there for help?"

"Never thought of it," Dave said evenly.

"Well, hell, let's get going," Larry said. "We kept Dave away from his wife long enough."

They made it back to Indian Tanks in three

days of steady riding. Dave seemed to pull in on himself as they neared the limestone potholes that dotted the small valley, many of which were fed by underground springs.

They pulled up at the lip of the valley. The slope shelved away from them toward a distant point that held a man's eye: a wagon parked under an unbrellalike oak.

A man in a straw hat, his age undetermined at this distance, was sitting on a stool a rifle across his knees. He seemed to be dozing. A girl was hanging clothes out on a line strung from the wagon to the tree.

Dave pointed away from the wagon. "That's it," he said tightly. "That's the herd I'm taking into Paradise Valley, Mr. Riley."

Jess stared.

He was conscious now of the sound he had been hearing but had not allowed to register: the distant baaing of sheep. Then his eyes made them out, scattered around the tanks and into the draws beyond — at least a thousand of them, he judged.

And he had made a promise to drive them into Paradise Valley!

V

For a long moment Jess Riley sat motionless, unbelieving. He had a cattleman's instinctive hatred of sheep and a Texan's low regard of the men who herded them. He had been born on a small Texas ranch and from the time he had been old enough to ride he had been around cows: the tough, wiry, mean-tempered Longhorns at first, tempered later by crossbreeding with Herefords. He knew cows as he knew horses and his life had been centered around both.

There were other ways to make a living, but for Jess Riley, raising beef was his.

The dirty gray balls of wool bunched at the far end of the valley assaulted his Texas sensibilities and anger built a fire in his gray eyes.

He swung around to face Dave, his voice harsh: "You told me you had a *herd* going up the Trail!"

Dave nodded. "I never said they were cows!" His voice was tight, his eyes guarded, studying Jess. "I figured it wouldn't matter . . ."

"You figgered wrong, mister!" Randy broke in grimly. He turned to Jess. "I knew there was something wrong with him from the beginning, Jess. The sonuvabitch tricked us!"

Jess saw Dave stiffen; he recognized the look that came into the sheepman's eyes and he quickly edged his mount in between Dave's and Randy.

"Easy, Randy. That kind of talk ain't called for!"

Randy started to say something, but Jess cut him off: "I said that's enough!"

Randy settled back in the saddle, his eyes

smoldering. Jess looked at Dave.

"You're right," he said coldly, "you didn't say what kind of herd. But you knew what I was thinking."

Dave shrugged. "Sure. But would you have given me a hand if I had told you right off they were sheep? Look," he went on defensively as Jess didn't immediately answer, "I'm sorry I misled you. But I was desperate. I was stuck here with fifteen hundred head . . ."

"Sheep!" Randy snarled the word at him.

Dave eyed him. "Yeah — sheep. Some day you might even get to appreciate them."

Jess cut in coldly: "You knew I was up the trail ahead of you?"

"I heard." Dave settled back in his saddle and shook his head. "I wasn't planning on your help; I knew how you'd feel. It wasn't easy, leaving my wife here, either. But I needed help and I went looking for it. I pay the same wages you do. The grub's no worse." His lips thinned and a bitter flame flickered in his eyes. "I found out sheepman is as dirty a word up here as it was in Texas. That's why I finally turned to you."

Jess shrugged. "I'm sorry, Dave." But there was little sympathy in his voice.

Dave swung around to the others. "I can't get through without help."

Randy sneered. The others shifted uncomfortably under Dave's scrutiny; they didn't say anything.

A hardness crept into Dave's eyes. "All right,"

33

he said finally. His voice was cold and remote. "I guess I was a fool to think you'd help."

He started to swing away, paused — and eyed Jess with cool challenge.

"You gave me your word, Jess. I'm sorry you're not man enough to live up to it."

The words stung. A flush crept into Jess's face as he watched Dave ride toward the camp below.

Randy shifted in his saddle, and said scornfully, "Hell with him, Jess." He glanced at his companions. "You heard him — he tricked us! We don't owe him a thing!"

Larry shrugged. "I don't know, Randy . . . he worked pretty hard for us . . ."

"Sure he did!" Randy bit out. "But that doesn't make me like him — or sheep, either!" He made a contemptuous motion downvalley. "Hell, you can smell them from here. They'd run us out of Texas if we showed up with the smell of mutton on us!"

Larry knuckled his chin stubble; he liked Dave. "Don't mind the sheep so much," he said. He looked at Jess. "I wish he had told us, though."

Hank spat a stream of tobacco juice on the ground. "Hate to see it turn out this way, Jess. But mebbe Randy's right."

"Reckon he is," Jess agreed. He was looking down to the sheep camp, to the small figure of a woman standing by a clothesline strung from the wagon to a tree branch. An old man in a straw hat, holding a shotgun loosely in his right hand, was watching from the side of the wagon.

A sense of shame touched him. He had given Dave his word: *sheep or cattle, what the hell did it matter?*

"I talked you into coming along," he said. "Can't say I blame any of you for turning back and heading for home."

Randy frowned. "What about you, Jess?"

Jess shrugged. "Reckon I'll ride along with Dave — see that he gets those sheep up to his place in Paradise Valley."

Hank worked his chaw around in his cheek. "Don't matter much to me, either way." He looked at Randy and shrugged. "I reckon I can stand the smell for a spell."

Chuck glanced at Bob Rich. They were of the same age and although they were not brothers, they had that same kind of closeness.

Chuck said, "I ain't in no hurry to get home."

Bob looked at Randy. "Guess I feel the same, Randy. I gave Dave my word . . ."

"You damn fools!" Randy shouted. "You know what will happen when we move those sheep toward those hills? That's cattle country up there! And some of those cattlemen are from Texas!"

"So I've heard," Jess said. "But Dave bought a ranch in that valley. I reckon he's entitled to run what he wants on it."

Randy settled back in the saddle. He knew Jess well enough to know the trail boss would go through with it. And he weighed his loyalty to this man against his contempt for the sheepman.

"All right," he gave in. "Count me in." His grin had a reckless twist to it. "I still don't like being tricked. And I don't give a damn about Dave. But it's gonna be interesting, trying to run a bunch of sheep past Texas cattlemen into Paradise Valley."

Dave Owens dismounted beside the woman and let his tired horse drift toward the wagon.

"That's the way it has to be, Luisa!" he said sharply. "Tell the old man!"

The girl's eyes flashed resentfully. She was slender, olive-skinned, dark-haired. Even drably dressed she looked beautiful. And she was spirited.

"You tell him!" she said angrily. "After all, he's your . . ."

"No!" he cut her off harshly. "You know how it is between us!"

She bit her lip. "All right," she assented reluctantly, "I'll tell him. But he won't understand."

He shrugged and turned to look back to the ridge; the Texans were riding down the slope toward them. A small smile of satisfaction wiped the harshness from his face.

"They're coming, Luisa. I knew they would."

"Texans!" Luisa's voice was distrustful. "Why should they help us — against their own kind?"

"The big one," Dave pointed out, "the man riding the bay horse. His name is Jess Riley. He'll get us and the sheep through."

The girl studied the oncoming riders for a moment; they were still too far away for her to make them out clearly. She shook her head.

"We should never have come here, Antonio."

"Dave!" he reminded her sharply. "It's Dave Owens! Remember that, Luisa!"

Her lips curled in bitter distaste. "Ah . . . I forgot. You are still ashamed of that name, as you were in Texas. What about me, then? How shall I be called? Maryann? Carolyn?"

He stiffened at the contempt in her voice. "It'll be what I say it is!" he said angrily. He glanced toward the oncoming riders. "One other thing. The old man — he works for us. A Mexican sheepherder — he doesn't speak English."

A defiant flush darkened Luisa's cheeks.

He went on coldly, before she could speak. "It's the way it has to be if we want to get through to Paradise Valley!"

He eyed the old man watching them from the scant shade of the wagon.

"Tell him, Luisa. He . . . he'll take it from you."

She nodded slowly, a hurt in her eyes now. "Yes . . . he'll take it." There was an ache in her voice, and a tenderness. "But he won't understand."

She turned to the wagon as Dave began to walk toward the oncoming riders.

VI

The sheep dogs came running up as Dave waited, jumping all over him, barking excitedly. They were glad to see him. He knelt in the dirt and roughed them up a bit, smiling.

"All right, Maria," he said to the white and tan dog, "I'm back. Now go back and keep an eye on the sheep."

The dog wagged her tail, her tongue lolling. She was a mixed breed of sheep dog, mostly Pyrrenean mixed with Scottish strain. She was intelligent, well trained, young enough to be frisky, and old enough to take her job seriously.

Dave called the other dog Baldo. Black and white, he was of the same breed, but older, heavier and more reserved in his affection.

Dave shoved him away with gentle push. "You, too, Baldo." There was genuine affection in his voice. "Go on . . . back to work."

The dogs started off, stopping to watch as Jess and his companions rode up to the camp.

Dave straightened and motioned them off. "Go on," he ordered. "They're friends."

The dogs took him at his word. They went bounding back to the sheep.

Jess' voice was short: "We've changed our minds. We'll give you a hand getting those sheep into Paradise Valley."

Dave hid the quick gleam that came into his eyes. "You don't have to," he said coldly. "I'll make out . . ."

"Aw, hell, Dave," Bob Rich cut in. "Don't get yore back up. Jess said we're gonna help."

"Sure," Larry grinned. "Let's get your sheep moving."

Jess was looking at the girl standing by the wagon. He said, "Your wife, Dave?"

Dave nodded. "Luisa." His voice was still stiff. "And my herder, Urquillo."

Jess touched his fingers to his hat brim. "Glad to see you're all right, Mrs. Owens. I was worried about you after Dave told us he left you here alone."

Luisa stiffened, her angry gaze darting to Dave. The old man slowly set his shotgun down against the wagon wheel and took out a corncob pipe. He was a short, powerful man, his brown face wrinkled by a lifetime spent in the open. There was an honest pride in the way he stood there, facing them. He could have been any-where between forty and sixty; time had left its signs of passage only in the wrinkles around his eyes, like rings in a tree stump.

"My wife does the cooking," Dave said. A slow smile broke the stiffness in his face. "Hope you all like mutton."

Chuck grinned. "After Hank's cooking, even mutton will be a relief."

Randy was eyeing the sheep at the far end of the valley.

"Don't look like too much of a job driving those sheep, Owens. With your herder and the dogs, you could have walked them into Paradise Valley easy."

"Could have," Dave admitted.

Randy's unfriendly gaze leveled on him. "What stalled you?"

"Paradise Valley ranchers."

Jess stirred in saddle. "They come this far out?"

Dave nodded. "A half-dozen riders from the Valley. They put some bullet holes through my wagon, shot a few sheep. Just a warning, they told me."

Randy shot a look at Jess. "I told you, Jess. It's guns he wanted, not drovers!"

The trail boss's gaze drifted to the girl by the wagon. She was watching them, a distrust in her eyes; there was the same look in the old man's gaze.

Dave said bitterly, "All I want is what is mine."

Randy leaned over his saddle horn. "You lied to us about your herd," he said contemptuously. "Maybe you're lying about your land, too."

Dave gave him a hard look. "Some day, mister . . ."

Jess said quietly, "It's a fair question."

Dave nodded. He walked to the wagon, took out a small iron box and lifted a manila envelope from it. He handed it to the trail boss.

"Bill of sale and deed to the Jenkins' place. All

legal. Recorded in the courthouse in Bentley. That's the town in Paradise Valley."

Jess glanced at the papers and handed them back. "I can understand the ranchers not wanting you in the valley," he said slowly. "But you could have gone to the law."

"I tried," Dave said harshly. "The sheriff ran me out of town."

Jess frowned. It was an old story; he had seen it happen in Texas. Right or wrong, most cattlemen feared sheep. They overgrazed the range, they multiplied faster than cows and they left an odor on the land that cattle shunned. Yet he knew there were places where cattlemen and sheepmen had learned to live together.

Hank said dryly over Jess's thoughts: "Sounds like a fair-minded sheriff." To Dave: "Who is he?"

Dave shrugged. "Man named Tennelly."

Hank straightened abruptly in his saddle. "Tennelly?" He shot a look at Jess.

Dave said, "Cal Tennelly. Tall, rangy man with sandy hair, a scar on his right cheek . . ."

Hank whistled softly. "Cal Tennelly wearing a badge." He spat tobacco juice onto the ground. "Times do change."

Dave said, "You know him?"

Hank looked at Jess — he nodded slowly. "We know him."

Dave's gaze went to Jess. "It's my land, my place! I've got as much right in Paradise Valley as they have!"

Jess grinned, but his eyes were bleak. "Can't argue against that." He turned to his companions. "Well, you heard him. Dave's got troubles. If we ride with him, we'll be part of it."

Larry Overton spat on the ground. He looked suddenly older, harder. "Never ran away from trouble in my life," he said.

Bob Rich glanced at Chuck. "Paradise Valley, eh?" He chuckled softly. "With a name like that I'm kinda looking forward to seeing the place."

Chuck grinned. "Must be something wrong, Jess — if Tennelly's the law up there."

The trail boss turned his attention back to Dave. "How fast can we move those sheep?"

"In this country, ten miles a day. Push them and maybe we can make fifteen. But they're stubborn. And it doesn't take much to panic them."

"Stampede?"

"Not like cattle," Dave said. "They'll run, but they won't scatter. Herd instinct. They'll stay together, following the leaders." He shrugged. "Even over a cliff, if they're headed that way."

Randy snorted.

Dave eyed him with glint of cold anger. "They're easier to handle than cows. All we have to do is keep the rams moving — and the dogs and I will see to that."

Jess put his glance on the distant hills. "Then we should make Santiago Pass in five days?"

Dave licked his lips. "If we don't get stopped first!"

The trail boss ran his hard glance over the sheepman. "I said we'd get your sheep into the valley. Let's get them moving!"

VII

The country beyond Indian Tanks sloped upward in gentle rises, crisscrossed by erosion gullies and deeper ravines. The graze was poor. The land was tinder dry and heat clung like a gray mist against the hills.

Luisa and Urquillo rode in the wagon, moving ahead of the sheep, pointing toward a camp site ahead.

Dave rode with the Texans. He had changed from the smiling, eager-to-please man they had known. He had taken a gunbelt from his blanket roll and strapped it around his waist. Both belt and gun, a Smith & Wesson .44, looked used. He seemed preoccupied now, a man weighed down by some private decision.

The Texans had little to do.

The dogs worked swiftly and efficiently, cutting back and forth, nagging when a ewe lagged behind, pulling back and crouching when a ram suddenly turned belligerent, lowering his horns. They remained just out of range then, waiting patiently until the ram lost interest and decided to move ahead.

During the noon break, while the sheep rested, Maria and Baldo stood guard, usually

43

from some vantage where they could keep an eye on the flock.

Still, it was slow going. The country became rougher, more brushy. The dogs had a harder time now, cutting back strays that wandered into wooded draws and keeping the rebellious rams headed in the right direction.

They made an estimated twelve miles the first day; they were up and moving before the sun rose the next morning. The land still slanted upward. Cotton puffs of cloud rimmed the horizon, but the sun still blazed out of a blue lead sky and no wind stirred the midday heat. And the distant hills appeared no nearer.

But they had left the area grazed over by the year's cattle drives north and the sheep were finding better feed. Water remained a problem. They were following a riverbed coursing down from the hills. The long drought had all but dried the stream's flow. Here and there, however, small brackish pools remained, guarded by angry gnats that hovered overhead.

Dave worked with the dogs, scouting out the strays, heading them away from poisonous lupine and choke-cherry.

Luisa and Urquillo took care of the lambs, carrying the weaker ones along in the wagon and doctoring the footsore with an old remedy of pine tar.

The Texans did what they could, riding herd on strays Dave and the dogs missed. But the work was unfamiliar and not to their liking.

Most of the men took it good-naturedly enough, but the strain between Randy and Dave grew more pronounced. Randy didn't like Dave, didn't trust him, and he was vocal in his dislike of sheep.

It was only a matter of time before things came to a head between them, Jess thought — and he knew no way to stop it.

He had his own doubts about the sheepman. Dave was an enigma. He kept to himself mostly. Jess sensed a hostility in the man, deep and guarded. He was sensitive about sheep — perhaps he had a right to be — but there was more to it than that. There was a resentment in him Jess caught at odd times when Dave didn't know Jess was watching him.

And something else bothered the big Texas trail boss. He didn't like the way Dave treated his wife. He seldom raised a hand to help her at night when the added burden of feeding six extra hungry Texans brought her to near exhaustion. Nor did Dave show any regard for his herder, Urquillo. Mostly he avoided the old man.

It disturbed Jess. He had committed himself to a man he couldn't understand and who he was beginning to dislike. But Dave had probably saved his life, he remembered, and hell, a man's relationship with his wife was his own business.

Noon of the third day found them heading

down a wide level valley. Suddenly the Paradise Hills loomed nearer, blue-black against the horizon. Santiago Pass was a dark slash at the base of the hills. The upper slopes were timbered. The air seemed clearer, a bit cooler. The riverbed ran deeper now and there was more water in it.

An old road, long out of use, came from the pass and angled across the valley. Jess, pulling up in the shade of a gnarled oak to light a cigarette, surveyed the distant hills. The bleating of the sheep filled the air. Most of the flock were lying down; a few ewes remained on their feet, nibbling at spiky growth.

Randy joined Jess under the tree. His face was flushed and there was disgust in his voice.

"Dumbest animals I ever herded," he commented loudly. Jess glanced in the direction Randy was looking and saw Dave riding toward them and knew that the time had come: that Randy had chosen this moment to push Dave to a showdown.

The others were converging toward them, a few yards behind the sheepman. He saw Dave react to Randy's words, his shoulders straightening.

Randy said, "You ride up to them and they just look you in the face, too dumb to run and too stupid to move. And the smell. . . ." He turned as Dave rode up, eyeing him with malicious expectancy. "Knew I smelled something. Thought it was one of your sheep."

46

Jess said sharply, "Randy!" But Dave edged between them, facing the red haired Texan, a cold smile on his face. The others, sensing trouble, pulled up behind Jess.

"You've got a loud mouth," Dave said. "I didn't like you the first time we met — I like you less now." He shook Jess's hand from his shoulder. "It's time we had it out," he said to Jess. "If we're going into Paradise Valley together, I want him off my back."

The effrontery of this man shocked Randy. He said harshly, "Why, you goddam sheepherder . . ." and dropped his hand to his gun — then froze, a small shock of surprise in his eyes. Dave's draw had been fast, smooth, and the muzzle that was aimed at Randy's middle was rock steady.

"I'm a sheepman," Dave said grimly. "Been one all my life. And I happen to think sheep are better than cows. They can live on less, get by on bad range, and they're not a one time crop, like cows. And I've had it up to here with your grousing." He handed Jess his gun and slid out of the saddle. "Maybe you can make me eat my words," he sneered to Randy.

A cocky grin twisted Randy's lips. He handed his gun to Bob Rich and wasted no time in going after Dave.

It was a vicious, no-holds-barred fight: slogging, brutal. They were evenly matched in size and weight and the battle see-sawed to an inconclusive finish.

Dave was on his knees, blood trickling from a corner of his mouth when Jess stopped it. Randy was trying to get up, but the effort, for the moment, was beyond him. His lower lip was cut and one eye was closed shut.

Jess pulled Dave to his feet. Blood was streaming from the sheepman's nose.

"Reckon you made your point," the trail boss said. He turned to Randy who was being helped by Larry. "What about you?"

Randy peered at Dave from his good eye. "Reckon he has," he admitted grudgingly. Then a smile twisted across his battered lips. "I take back half of what I said about sheepherders."

"And the other half?"

Randy shrugged. "We'll see."

Dave pulled himself into saddle. He swayed a little, but waved Bob Rich away as the young cowboy moved to help. He looked at Jess.

"We'll be camping at the mouth of Santiago Pass tomorrow night," he said. It was an effort to talk, but his gaze was level and hard. "If we're going to have trouble, that's where we'll get it!"

He turned his mount away and rode off.

The Texans grouped around Randy. Bob Rich looked after Dave. "Thought he was an easy-going cuss." He grinned. "Sure changed my thinking in a hurry." He turned to Jess. "See the way he drew on Randy?"

Jess nodded slightly.

Hank scratched in his chin whiskers. "That ain't the Dave Owens I knew."

"Yeah," Jess said, his eyes on the sheepman fading in the distance. "He's changed." He turned to Randy. "How do you feel?"

It pained Randy to smile. It hurt him more to admit what he had to.

"Take it all back . . . about sheepherders." He massaged his jaw. "About Dave, anyway."

He pulled himself up into the saddle, took the gun Rich handed him and slid it into his holster. Looking off in the direction Dave had ridden, an irrepressable grin lighted his good eye. "Hell," he said good-naturedly, "if Dave can stand these damn sheep, I reckon I can."

VIII

The sheep wagon pulled up at the edge of a wooded draw where a trickle of water flowed between sand-scoured rocks, falling and gurgling softly in the afternoon stillness. Insects hummed over the shallow pools. Birds chirped busily in the trees, darting restlessly among the branches.

Riding on the seat beside Urquillo, Luisa felt depressed. They had left the sheep and the Texans behind; it would be dark before they caught up.

She sat motionless, staring off into the distance, eyes half-closed, a great weariness pinning her to the seat.

Urquillo sensed her mood. A sadness crept into his gaze. He was a man not given to talk;

sheepherders learned to live with silence.

"You worry, Luisa?" He spoke with an accent; it was not the tongue he was born with.

Shame burned in Luisa's cheeks. "A . . . a servant," she said softly. "How can you stand it?"

Urquillo shrugged. "It is of no matter."

She turned to face him. "How can you say that? Your own son . . ."

He cut her off sharply: "It does not matter!"

He climbed down from the wagon and began unhitching the team.

"Come," he said, but his voice was gentle now, understanding. "We have work to do, Luisa."

She sighed. Years of compliance brought her down from the wagon and set her to making camp. She moved listlessly. The days had become blurs of memory, melting one into another: days of chores, of cooking and washing, of aching muscles and restless sleep.

She had been a happy child, but now only occasionally did she remember those days. It seemed she had lived forever in this wagon, jolting along trackless paths, following behind mindless sheep until she, too, became unthinking and unfeeling.

Locked inside a small hidebound chest in the wagon were her meager personal belongings; locked there, too, were her hopes and her dreams.

Urquillo unhitched the team and came back to give her a hand with the heavy iron stew pot, setting it up for the night's meal. A flash of resentment burned briefly in her: six more mouths to feed! How easily Dave had shifted this extra burden onto her.

She paused to look off toward the hills. They were less than a day's march away now. Paradise Valley lay just beyond. . . .

Urquillo saw the look in her eyes. "You are tired, Luisa. It is hard on you, I know." He put a hand on her shoulder. "But soon now we shall be home."

"Home?" There was a bitterness in her voice.

"A fine place," the old man said. "There — just beyond those hills." An ache crept into his voice. "A place to grow old . . . some day even, God willing, to play with my grandchildren."

She was silent, staring off.

He picked up his axe and went into the draw where dead branches had piled up during winter runoffs. He was a man used to work and loneliness; his dreams were of practical things and not beyond achieving.

He returned with an armful of wood and dumped it by the iron pot. Luisa had not moved while he was gone, but he understood. He set about making a fire and drawing water.

The shadows began to steal across the camp, filling the narrowing end of the valley.

Urquillo paused to rest for a few moments, filling his old corncob pipe. He puffed silently for a while, then, disturbed by Luisa's mood, he went to her.

"You are worried still about Antonio?"

She nodded. "It is wrong, what he is doing. Lying to those men . . . about you and me."

"Perhaps he is right, Luisa — it is the way it has to be." He shrugged. "I don't care what he has told them — all I care about is getting home."

"You can call it home?" she asked bitterly. "A place we have never seen?"

His eyes were grave as he looked toward the darkening hills. "Antonio has seen it — he said it was a fine place for us." He was silent for a moment, then his voice gentled: "We can't go on forever, Luisa, driving our sheep over land that is not ours."

"And what if we do get through?" she asked. "Texans drove us out of our last home. Texans in Paradise Valley will be no different."

"We'll see," Urquillo said, his voice harsh. But Luisa's question had unsettled him. He clamped his teeth on the stem of his pipe and strode off.

Luisa looked down the long valley where sheep and riders could now be seen moving slowly toward them. The Texans rode together, she noticed, a clannish bunch; she could make out the tall figure of Jess Riley among them.

"Yes," she murmured bitterly, "we shall see."

Night drew a dark blanket over the hills, softening their outline. The campfire flickered cheerfully, casting dancing shadows over the canvas side of the wagon.

Luisa dished out mutton stew from the iron pot, and homemade sourdough biscuits. There was a strained reserve about her that the Texans sensed and understood. They took their rations and retired to their camp some distance off; a man and his wife ought to have some privacy.

Urquillo ate quickly, then with Baldo at his heels and his shotgun in hand, he disappeared into the darkness to stand first watch over the sheep.

Dave fed scraps to Maria who bedded down under the wagon. Luisa, eating last, watched him.

"You've been fighting again?"

He straightened and looked at her. The right side of his face was swollen and his ribs ached. He smiled, although it was an effort to do so.

"The redheaded Texan," he said "I gave as good as I got." There was an edge of pride in his voice that Luisa sensed and understood.

She went to him, touching the bruises on his face. "Why, Antonio? Why does it have to be like this . . . always a chip on your shoulder . . . always fighting?"

His eyes went hard, but he didn't answer. He knelt again to fondle Maria, scratching behind her ears.

Luisa's glance dropped to the gun on his hip. "The gun," she said, "is that necessary, too? Must you . . . ?"

He turned, cutting her off with a curt reply: "I

told you when we left Texas it was going to be different."

"You were almost killed then," she pointed out.

He straightened, smiling — but there was a chill in his eyes that frightened her.

"I learned," he said coldly, "many things since then."

"Is that why you've called yourself Dave Owens?"

He shrugged. "It's an easy name to remember."

She bit her lips, resenting his easy explanation and yet worrying about him. "You're ashamed of me, aren't you? Of Urquillo, too?"

He studied her for a long moment, his eyes hard. "I learned my lesson well, Luisa. You go with the ways of the country — or you don't survive!"

She watched him take a lantern from the wagon and stride off toward the Texan camp. Loneliness made a small hard knot in her stomach.

It was two years since her mother died: the last truly gentle voice she remembered. She was starved for something she could not quite understand. In his way Urquillo loved her, but neither he nor Dave needed her. Both men were fixed on a course of their own — both were stubborn men — and the long tension she had been living with finally brought tears to her eyes.

Turning blindly she crawled inside the wagon and wept.

The Texans looked up as Dave joined them, his lantern casting a circle of light over their camp.

"Anybody feel lucky?" Dave produced a deck of cards. "I don't feel sleepy."

Hank grinned. "I got a few pesos burning a hole in my pocket."

The others felt the same way.

Chuck said, "Quarter limit, Dave. I want to get home with *some* money."

Larry spread his blanket on the ground between them. Dave placed the deck down in the middle of it. "High card deals?"

The others agreed. Randy glanced at the trail boss who was standing off to one side, smoking a cigar. There was a somber look in Riley's eyes.

"You in, Jess?"

Jess shook his head. He could see Luisa now, coming out of the wagon. She brushed her eyes as though she had been crying.

Standing here, a few yards apart from his companions, he felt the run of his own loneliness. All his life he had worked hard, before and after his parents had died. He, like most of the people he knew, had wanted nothing more than a ranch of his own: to be his own man, and not have to spend his years hiring out to others. And now, suddenly, he was aware of the years that had slipped by. He was nearly thirty and he had his ranch — *and he had nothing else!*

There was more to living than this, he knew; and the faces of girls he had known drifted through his thoughts, leaving behind an emptiness that depressed him.

Randy said, "Come on, Jess — loosen up." He chuckled, although it hurt his face to do so. "Between us we could take Dave for everything he owns, including his damn sheep."

Jess shook his head again irritably. He could see Luisa struggling with the heavy iron pot and a small anger came to him at Dave's lack of consideration for his wife.

Dave glanced at the big trail boss as Jess strode off. A glint appeared in his eyes, but his tone was affable as he turned back to the others.

"Five card stud," he said. "Keep us all honest."

Luisa was lifting the pot back into the wagon when Jess came up. He took it from her and placed it inside.

"Heavy work for a woman," he said.

She turned away from him, not wanting him to see her eyes, knowing they were puffed, resenting this weakness in her.

"I can manage," she said coldly. "It's my job."

He felt her distance, and it bothered him.

"Not much of a life for a woman, having to live out of a wagon like this. And having to feed six extra men doesn't help." He was trying to be kind. "One of my men is a cook — I could get him to give you a hand."

"Don't bother." Her voice was sharp as she turned away from him, toward the fire. Then she paused and looked back, her manner softening.

"I'm sorry. I didn't mean to be rude. And — thanks for offering." She motioned toward the coffee pot. "Coffee?"

He joined her, hunkering down on the other side of the dying fire. She poured him a cup.

"We'll be in Paradise Valley in a couple of days," he said. "You must be looking forward to getting settled again."

She shrugged, uncaring.

He misunderstood her gesture. "Are you worried, Mrs. Owens?"

She looked at him across the fire, her eyes dark and unreadable. "No," she said. Her voice was without emotion. "I'm not worried, Mr. Riley. I just don't care what happens anymore."

He frowned. "I know there's bad feeling in the valley about your husband settling there. That's why we're here, Mrs. Owens."

"Why?" Her voice cut coldly across his. "Why should you help us?"

He was unsettled by the hostility in her voice.

"Didn't your husband tell you, Mrs. Owens?"

"Husband?" Her eyes held a flash of resentment. Then: "Oh, yes . . . he did say something about you returning a favor."

Jess was silent for a moment, sipping his coffee. The undercurrents in this woman's voice bothered him.

"You don't like Texans, do you, ma'am?"

"I was born in Texas," she replied. "My mother died there."

She stood up and emptied the dregs of the coffee pot over the embers. The fire hissed and a small cloud of steam escaped into the night.

She said, "If you don't mind, I think I'll go to bed."

He got to his feet. "Thanks for the coffee, Mrs. Owens."

Her eyes darkened with some secret displeasure. "My name is Luisa," she said. And then, almost as though driven by some inner malice, "I'm Mexican. And a sheepman's daughter," Her smile was still on her lips. "Doesn't it bother you, Mr. Riley?"

He looked at her, his gaze level, probing. "Why should it?"

Her defenses sagged. For a brief moment her aching loneliness shone through.

She said quietly, "Good night, Mr. Riley."

He watched her walk to the rear of the wagon. "Good night, Luisa."

She flashed him a small, grateful smile before climbing inside. Jess waited by the dead embers of the supper fire, smoking the last of his cigar. His eyes were thoughtful as he turned back to his Texas camp.

IX

Luisa was up early the next morning, preparing breakfast while Urquillo went down into the draw for firewood. His axe, ringing out in the cool dawn air, roused the sleeping men in the Texas camp.

Dave sat on the wagon tongue, watching Luisa. He had just come in from the late night watch; he looked surly, hard, the stubble on his face grown darker with each passing day.

He said, finally, "What did he want, Luisa?"

She was mixing a batch of biscuits in the bowl set on the tailgate of the wagon. She eyed him questioningly.

"The big Texan? Riley?" Her lips curled in a small smile. "I see it bothers you."

He said insistently, "What did he want?"

Her eyes clashed with his. "He was kind and considerate . . . something you seem not to have learned."

"Well, well." Dave came up off the wagon tongue and walked to her. "So he's interested in you? That'll help."

"Help?" Her voice cut at him. "I'm your wife. That's what you told him, isn't it?"

He shrugged carelessly. "Seemed the best thing, at the time." He glanced toward the draw where Urquillo was still chopping wood. "How's the old man taking it?"

"Why don't you ask him?" she snapped. "He's your father, too!"

Dave reacted to the anger in her voice. "What I'm doing is for all of us," he said. "Some day you and the old man will understand."

He whistled to the dogs lying under the wagon. They joined him, tails wagging, eager to start the day's work.

"Where are you going?"

"Get the sheep moving. I'll be back for breakfast."

"We're about out of flour," she said. "And most other staples, too." There was a sudden tiredness in her voice that held him. He smiled. "I know, sis . . . it's rough. Make out a list. I'll ride into town as soon as I can."

Fear flashed into her eyes. "No . . . not alone! You know what those men said . . ."

He cut her off. "No one's going to stop me, Luisa!" He dropped his hand to his gun, his eyes hard. "No one!"

She watched him stride off, alarmed and afraid. She no longer knew her brother, she thought dismally. She had seen him change, from the day they had been driven out of Texas.

She avoided Jess Riley at breakfast. The Texans ate quickly and rode off. They were used to early morning riding, and although driving sheep was not the same as herding cattle, they felt comfortable in this routine.

She heard them banter among themselves as they went off. She envied their comraderie, their easy self-assurance.

And she hated them for it.

The valley narrowed, funneling toward the break in the hills that made a wall against the horizon. The sheep spilled like some dirty gray puddle over the land, the rams moving with majestic slowness, curved horns ready to challenge any predator. The ewes and the lambs tagged along behind.

The Texans rode together for the most part, splitting occasionally to turn back some stubborn sheep the dogs missed.

On one such occasion Randy rode up to a draw and looked down, his face mirroring disgust. He turned and waved his hat to Jess who swung around and joined him.

"Look," Randy pointed. "Damn fool animal can't even get up by herself."

One of the ewes had tumbled down the draw and landed on its back The heavy, matted fleece made it difficult for her to get back on her feet. She made a ludicrous sight, pipestem legs kicking futilely in the air.

Dave and the others rode up. The Texans watched as Dave dismounted, went down into the draw and flipped the animal back onto its feet. The ewe scrambled up the bank, bleating her displeasure.

One of the dogs chased her back to the main flock moving steadily toward the pass.

Hank wiped his face with his neckerchief. The day was hot and getting sticky. He glanced at the dark clouds beginning to boil up over the hills.

"Glory be," he said fervently, "if it doesn't look like we're finally gonna get some rain."

Dave eyed the clouds with worried gaze. "Hate to get caught out here when it breaks." He turned to look at the sheep moving slowly ahead.

"We'll have to push them, Jess. I want to make the pass before dark."

The wagon broke down in the afternoon. One of the front wheels hit an imbedded rock and several old spokes splintered. The wagon sagged sharply, throwing Luisa against Urguillo who was driving.

They climbed down and surveyed the damage. They were less than two miles from the pass. The sheep were still several miles behind.

While Liusa unhitched the team and led them into the shade of some nearby trees, Urquillo set about unfastening the spare wheel lashed under the wagon. Then he went back under the trees and found a long branch which he trimmed with his axe into a stout pole.

Jess Riley rode up as the old man slid the pole under the wagon and started to raise it. He was a solid man, stronger than he looked.

Luisa was standing by the tailgate. She turned as Jess rode up and dismounted, then looked quickly away, not wanting him to see the quick flush of pleasure that came into her face. She was finding herself drawn to this big, considerate Texan with the quiet voice — drawn more than she cared to admit to herself.

Jess said to her, "I saw you were in trouble." He went to Urquillo, laying a gentle hand on his shoulder. "Let me give you a hand, old man."

Urquillo shook him off. "I fix," he said coldly.

"And I am Urquillo, not old man!"

Jess responded to the rebuke in the sheepherder's voice: "Sorry, Urquillo. Dave told me, but I forgot."

"Dave?" Urquillo's dark eyes leveled on Jess. "I know nobody by that name."

Jess stepped back, frowning. A faint pulse of anger beat at his throat at this old man's stubbornness.

Luisa came up, speaking quickly: "Urquillo . . . he only wants to help." She turned to Jess. "He . . . he's been with us a long time . . . he's used to doing things himself."

Jess glanced at the gathering thunderheads. A streak of lightning made a jagged path over the hills.

He nodded to Luisa, then turned to Urquillo. "Look," he said easily. "I'm sorry I hurt your feelings. But getting that wagon rolling again is a two-man job, and I don't think we've got time to argue." He put his right arm under the pole and gently shoved the older man away. "Go on — get that wheel on."

His tone was gentle but firm. Urquillo scowled. Luisa put a hand on his arm. "Please?"

He eyed the big Texan for a long moment; there was a deep pride in this man that was not to be taken lightly.

Jess smiled. "Come on, Urquillo . . . we're all in this together."

A flicker passed through Urquillo's eyes. He nodded and turned to the wagon. He worked

63

quickly, tugging the broken wheel off its axle, laying it aside. He greased the axle and the hub of the spare wheel, slid it on and secured it.

Jess eased the wagon front down, tossing the pole aside. Urquillo was fastening the broken wheel under the wagon.

Jess said to Luisa, "What did he mean, he didn't know anybody by the name of Dave?"

Luisa hesitated; she was a bad liar and it showed. "I don't know." She turned away from the big trail boss to look at the clouds massed over Paradise Hills. "Do you think it will rain down here?"

Jess shrugged. He was aware she knew more than she was willing to say, but he did not press her.

"Can't tell," he replied offhand. "I've seen clouds like that sail overhead without spilling a drop only to dump a cloudburst on folks fifteen miles further on."

He walked to his horse and paused. After a moment he looked back to her. He said quietly, "Something wrong between you and Dave?"

The question unsettled her and brought a stiffness to her voice.

"Why?"

He shrugged, finding it hard to shape his answer. He was a man not glib and easy with women, and she attracted him deeply — and he felt disturbed and guilty because of it.

"A man generally sleeps with his wife," he said

bluntly. "I've noticed Dave rolls up in his bedroll by the fire."

Color spotted Luisa's cheeks and the stiffness spread to her face. "Mr. Riley," she said coldly, "I don't think it's any of your business where Dave sleeps."

"It isn't," Jess agreed somberly. He mounted then and looked down at her and was silent for a long moment. Then a small sigh gusted out of him, and he said what he had to.

"I don't know about Dave. But if you were my woman I wouldn't sleep by the fire." He touched fingers to his hat brim. "Good day, Mrs. Owens."

He jerked his big bay horse around, sent it off at a gallop. Luisa stood still, her body straight and stiff, watching him. A tremor went through her.

Urquillo, watching from the far side of the wagon, put his old corncob between his stubby teeth, but he did not light it. Then, as Luisa did not move, he walked around to her.

"Come," he said. "It is time to go."

She didn't hear him, or if she did it made no impression.

He looked after Jess, his brown face impassive. "Some day he will have to know, Luisa."

She nodded, but her gaze remained on Jess's diminishing figure.

"What will you do then?"

She turned now, eyeing the old sheepherder with quick apprehension. "Do?"

65

He put a callused hand on her arm. "I've seen the look in your eyes." He shook his head. "He is a good man. I feel that. But . . . remember, Luisa . . . he is a Texan."

She flashed him a look as she turned, climbing into the wagon. *Yes,* she thought bitterly, *he is a Texan. And Texans don't marry daughters of Mexican sheepmen!*

X

The wagon was parked just off the old wagon road coming out of Santiago Pass when the welcoming committee from Paradise Valley came riding up, scattering the bedded sheep before them, sending them running in panic-stricken flight into the gullies and ravines that slanted down from the mountains.

Luisa and Urquillo were by the campfire, getting things ready for supper. The sun, setting behind them, cast a strange glow against the dark clouds over the hills.

Dave had gone with the Texans down the creek to wash accumulated dust and grime from their beard-stubbled faces. The storm over Paradise Valley had lulled them and they were not expecting trouble this night.

The riders were lean, tough, insolent: a half-dozen of them, all under thirty — ranch hands who hated sheep because they worked for men who hated sheep.

They rode roughshod through the flock, shooting a few that got in their way. But their main target was the sheep wagon under the trees.

The leader was a curly-haired, rangy man with a Colt thonged down on his right hip, gunfighter style. There was a bronco streak in Clay Hollister; in his earlier years it had gotten him into trouble. Now he was more careful. But he had picked the men who rode with him for that same wild streak — and he knew how to manage them.

"We'll teach that goddamn sheepherder a real lesson this time," he yelled to his companions.

Baldo and Maria were under the wagon as the riders came toward them. Baldo went charging for the dark shapes looming up and one of the riders shot him, the bullet glancing off Baldo's ribs, knocking him down.

Urquillo grabbed his shotgun and Luisa, shaken and frightened, grabbed his arms. He fired, but the buckshot charge blasted harmlessly into the air as the Paradise Valley riders loomed up.

The rider just ahead of Clay, a sandy-haired, arrogant youngster named Les Cantry, palmed his Colt and slammed it contemptuously across Urquillo's head. The sheepman staggered and went down to his knees, blood streaming from the gash in his scalp.

Luisa stepped in front of him as one of the other riders raised his gun. Clay said sharply, "Hell . . . not the woman, Nick!"

The man turned, grinning, and fired twice through the canvas sides of the wagon — then whirled as Dave, running ahead of the others, came into the fireglow.

Luisa saw him first. She flung herself at him as he raised his Colt. He tried to brush her aside. Clay deliberately ran his horse into both of them, knocking them down. Dave's Colt flew out of his hand. Clay jammed the muzzle of his rifle between Dave's shoulder blades as he started to get up.

"Wal, now," he drawled, his voice easy, contemptuous. "If it ain't the sheepherder, packin' a gun." He grinned at his companions clustered behind him. "A real bad man."

Les Cantry said grimly, "Hell, Clay, shoot him and get it over with. I'll burn the wagon."

He started to slide out of saddle but stopped as a cold voice cut at him from the shadows beyond the fire.

"You stay where you are! *All of you!*"

Les' surprised gaze went out to the men moving into the firelight. He counted six of them. Rifles glinted against the darkness.

Clay eased his rifle muzzle from Dave's back, allowing the sheepman to get to his feet. Luisa had gone to stand beside Urquillo, leaning dazedly against the tailgate. Her eyes were dark with horror.

Clay said stiffly to Dave, "I see you hired yourself some help. Won't do you any good, though. . . ."

His voice trailed off as Jess came full into the firelight. His Colt was still in his holster, but behind him his companions were shadowy, armed figures.

"Hello, Clay."

Clay leaned forward in saddle, peering at the big man on the other side of the fire. His thoughts slipped uncomfortably back to Texas, to thickets along the banks of the Nueces, to a small branding fire. . . .

Jess helped him out. "Still mavericking other men's cows, Clay?"

A small sigh gusted out of Clay. "Jess Riley!"

Les Cantry didn't know Jess, and he was the sort who wouldn't have cared. He dropped his palm to his holstered gun.

"Big man," he sneered. "Who is he, Clay?"

Clay Hollister didn't answer. His gaze slipped past Jess to the men behind him.

"Heard you were trailing a mixed herd to King City." His voice was tight. "What are you doing here?"

Jess said, "Helping a man get his sheep to his ranch."

Les swung around to look at Hollister. "You mean . . . they're Texans?"

Hollister nodded.

Jess said dryly, "That bother you, son?"

Les eased around to face the big trail boss, his slim body tensing.

"I don't know who you are, mister. But if you're riding with this sheepherder, you ain't

69

Texan! Not in my book."

Hollister said sharply, "Easy, Les!"

"Easy, hell!" Les snapped. He eyed Jess, a sneer spreading across his reckless face. "Christ, you even smell of sheep."

He drew then, his hand coming up fast with his gun. Jess fired, knocking him out of the saddle.

The men behind Les kept their hands in plain sight. They glanced at Hollister, their eyes hard, questioning. They had not come expecting this kind of trouble.

Dave lunged for his Colt. Jess came around the fire and shouldered him away.

"Hold it, Dave! There won't be any more shooting tonight!"

Dave turned on him, eyes flaring, a murderous look in his face. "They're the ones, Jess."

Jess said flatly, "I said enough, Dave!"

Dave bent under the trail boss's stare; he took a deep breath and slipped his Colt back into holster.

Jess Riley moved from the wounded man lying on the ground to Hollister.

"Who sent you, Clay?"

Hollister eyed him in sullen anger. "Ranchers in Paradise Valley."

Jess thumbed back the hammer of his Colt. "Who sent *you?*"

"Lou Bretman, owns the B-In-A-Box spread. I work for him."

Jess' gaze ranged over the others. "Them too?"

Clay nodded, his mouth dry. "All except Les." He looked down at the wounded man. "He rides for Ned Sparrow."

Jess stepped back, motioning to Cantry who was sitting up, only half-conscious. "Better get him to a doctor."

Clay slipped out of the saddle. He bent over Les, helping him to his feet.

"Think you can ride, Les?"

The young cowpuncher nodded, biting his lips. The wound was high up in his right shoulder; his right hand hung nerveless, blood beginning to drip from his fingertips.

Luisa came up beside Jess. "He'll bleed to death before he gets back," she said.

The big Texan looked at her, his lips thinning to cold smile. "That's his worry, ma'am."

"No . . . no." She looked at Clay. "At least let me put a bandage on him?"

Hollister looked at Jess. There was a grim silence in the night and over it came the distant roll of thunder. Jess shrugged. "More than he deserves," he said, and moved back to the fire, hunkering down to watch.

Dave said roughly, "Hell with him, Luisa," and when she turned angrily on him he growled, "He tried to kill Jess, didn't he? And look what he did to Urquillo!"

Hollister was eyeing the Texans across the fire. He said brittlely, "We'll patch him up,

71

ma'am." Then, stiffly: "Thanks for offering."

He motioned a pock-faced young rider down from his horse. "Give me a hand, Nick."

Between them they got Cantry up into his saddle. But the man was too weak to hang on.

Clay glanced toward the hills. A cool wet wind rustled through the trees. The pass was shrouded in darkness, and high up the blackness flared as lightning tore it apart.

It was going to be a hell of a night, he thought. Anger made its brief and futile run through him.

He said, "Take my horse, Nick," and climbed up behind Cantry. He held the sagging man in his right arm and picked up the reins with his left.

Cantry stirred. He looked down at Jess by the fire, his eyes pained. What he saw was a blur, but pride and arrogance put a momentary challenge in his words: "I'll see you . . . again . . . mister."

Then Hollister whirled away, the others falling in behind. Jess watched them fade into the night. He stirred then, throwing a piece of wood into the fire as he straightened.

"All right, boys," he said, and waited as Hank, Randy and the others came toward him.

XI

The rain came a little later. It came in big drops at first, slapping through the trees, drumming against the canvas top of the sheep wagon. The fire hissed and spluttered.

The Texans brought out their ponchos. It was a protection of sorts, but they were used to this kind of hardship and no one complained.

Luisa tended to Urquillo. She got a bandage around his head and tried to get him to lie down inside the wagon. He refused. He kept looking at the big Texas trail boss, a strangeness in his eyes.

Maria was under the wagon, Her tail wagged and thumped nervously as she came out to stand beside Dave and looked off into the darkness. A whine issued from the sheep dog's throat.

Dave said, "Where's Baldo?"

Luisa's face crumpled and she motioned off into the night.

Dave said grimly: "Come on, Maria . . . let's find him." And with the dog at his heels he strode off into the blackness.

She looked after him, the rain beating on her face, soaking through her dress. Lightning flared viciously, outlining her against the wagon.

Jess Riley's big shadowy shape loomed up beyond the sputtering fire. He said gently, "You better get inside the wagon, Mrs. Owens."

She turned and stared numbly at him as he took her by the arm and pulled her toward the wagon. She balked now, turning. Her voice was flat and without emotion.

"No. I have to get supper."

"Not tonight," Jess said firmly. "No one's hungry anyway."

She looked deep into his face now, still

stunned by the violence of the past hour. She tried to find the hard-faced man who had shot Cantry but now there was only a tiredness in Jess' eyes and concern for her.

The rain slid cold fingers down her back. She shivered and hugged herself, an unconscious gesture. But she resisted as Jess pushed her toward the wagon.

Jess said impatiently, "You're a stubborn woman, Mrs. Owens," and swept her up in his arms, walking to the tailgate with her. She did not resist. She lay against him, her face close to his. Her hand reached up to touch his face.

"Jess. . . ."

He paused, suddenly conscious of what he was doing. He eased her down, but she clung to him, her eyes soft and caring. Her fingers went to his face, caressing. . . .

"Jess. . . ."

And then Dave came striding back into the flickering firelight. He paused as he saw them, the wounded sheep dog in his arms, Maria at his heels . . . and for a moment no one moved and a distorted sort of silence intruded upon the falling rain.

Then Luisa pushed away from Jess and ran to Dave. "How is he?" Her hand touched the sheep dog lying quiet in Dave's arms.

Dave's dark gaze lay on Jess' shadowy figure by the tailgate. He said tonelessly, "Not too bad. Bullet across his ribs."

The dog raised his head and whined as Luisa

caressed him. Maria began to bark excitedly and Jess drifted over. His voice was distant.

"Maybe you can talk your wife into getting in out of the rain," he said, and started to turn away.

Dave said quietly, "Just a minute, Jess," and when the Texan looked at him, he added, "I want to talk to you."

A cold smile pulled at the trail boss' lips; he said, "Sure." He misread the anxiety that flashed through Luisa's gaze.

Baldo stirred and licked Luisa's hand. She said to Dave, "Bring him to the wagon. I'll take care of him."

Jess waited. Luisa climbed into the wagon, pulling the canvas flap aside. A small yellow glow from a lamp inside slanted weakly through the falling rain. Dave handed the sheep dog up to her and she withdrew, the canvas flap falling back into place.

Jess' gaze slid to Urquillo. The old sheepman was hunkered down by the wagon, taking the rain stoically, an old blanket draped serape style across his shoulders.

Dave came back to join Jess by the fire. He knuckled his jaw, his gaze slanting away from the big Texan, into the dying blaze.

"Hell of a night," he murmured, and then turned and looked full into Jess Riley's face. "Luisa's a damned attractive woman," he said carefully.

"She is," Jess agreed, and waited, letting the

silence run between them. But Dave seemed content to let it go at this and it faintly angered and disturbed the big Texan.

He said bluntly, "None of my business, Dave. But a man oughta spend more time with his wife." And then, letting his anger show: "It's a hell of a lonely life for a woman."

Dave's smile showed his white teeth. "I guess you're right, Jess." He glanced toward the wagon. "I'll make it up to her when we get settled."

He rubbed his palm down over the wet shiny butt of his Colt, his voice casual. "You sure made the difference tonight, Jess — the way you handled those Paradise Valley cowpokes."

Jess's gaze made its quick search of Dave's face. For whatever reason, he thought coldly, Dave was overlooking the scene between him and his wife. He shrugged, falling in with Dave's attitude.

"How're the sheep?"

"Scattered up and down the gullies," Dave repined, "far as I can make out." A glint came into his eyes and his voice went grim: "They shot some."

Jess said, "You still want to go through with it?"

Dave's head jerked around and his gaze locked on the big Texas trail boss. He said harshly, "You're not quitting on me now, Jess?"

"I was thinking of your wife," Jess said evenly.

"Someone got hurt tonight. It could have been Mrs. Owens."

"I don't want Luisa hurt, either," Dave said grimly. "But I've come this far . . . I'm not turning back!"

He was silent a moment, something dark and hating making its run through him as he looked off into the night, toward the valley beyond the mountains. Lightning flared again, but it was distant now and the hard patter of rain began to diminish.

He turned back to Jess then, rain streaking down across his dark, stubbled face. "They ran me out of town, Jess," he said softly. "Called me a goddamn sheepherder . . . and other things. The sheriff did . . . and he had the town behind him . . . and the cattlemen backing him." He shook his head, the drops spraying outward from his hat brim. "I was run off my place once before. But not this time, Jess . . ." his voice fell off, hard and wicked, "not this time."

Jess shrugged. "I know how you feel." He was silent a moment, trying to sort out his thoughts . . . he was committed to this man, but he felt a dark undercurrent of purpose in this sheepman he couldn't understand.

"Did Jenkins know you were going to run sheep on his place when he sold out to you?"

Dave's eyes narrowed. "Does it matter?"

"In a way." Jess' gaze leveled on him. "I like a man who puts all his cards on the table."

Dave's grin was quick, easy. "Yes," he said. "Jenkins knew."

"And he still sold out to you?"

Dave nodded. "He was an irascible old buzzard . . . maybe he just wanted to get back at his neighbors. I guess he had other troubles, too. He didn't have too much stock on his place and he was losing what he had. That's what he told me."

Jess frowned. "Rustling?"

Dave shrugged. "I didn't ask — I didn't care about his problems. He was a sly man . . . he didn't say much. He was glad to leave and he sold out cheap, lock, stock and barrel."

"Stock, too?"

"What there was of it. I don't know what's left." He ran his palm down over the shiny wet butt of his Colt; it was the instinctive gesture of a man not to be put off. "It's my place, Jess. I'm going to settle there, come hell or high water!"

Jess nodded. "No reason why you shouldn't. I'll ride up in the morning. Maybe a little commonsense talk, instead of guns . . ."

Dave cut in: "I tried talking . . ."

"Maybe I'll do better," Jess cut him off. "I don't know Lou Bretman and Ned Sparrow. But I knew John Hendrix. A fair man. I'll talk to him."

The rain continued for a half-hour after that and then petered off. Lightning flickered fitfully for most of the night, but the thunder roll was faint and moving off into the distance.

The runoff from the mountains flooded the creek, the sound of rushing water pounding against the night. The Texans dozed fitfully, enduring the discomfort, knowing there was little they could do about it.

Jess stirred once and looked toward the wagon, a shapeless bulk under the dripping trees. The fire had gone out. Urquillo had crawled under the wagon, his usual sleeping place. Jess did not see Dave and the thought came to him that he must have joined Luisa in the wagon. He pushed the thought from him and closed his eyes, but it was a long time before he fell asleep.

Luisa was up and moving with the first light. She had changed into dry clothes, brushed her hair and tied it back on her neck with a bright yellow ribbon.

Rain still dripped softly from the trees, but the sky overhead was clear and there was a freshness to the morning, a clean fragrance that lifted her spirits and put a buoyancy in her movements.

Urquillo joined her, rolling stiffly from his bedroll under the wagon, a stoic, silent man. He had stored firewood under the wagon, covered by a small tarp, before the storm broke. He used this to get a fire going and a coffee pot bubbling.

It was the smell of coffee that woke the Texans. Hank crawled out of his bedroll and stretched in the morning brightness, his old bones creaking.

Randy, sitting up a few yards away, ran his fingers through his tousled hair. "You sound like a spavined mule, Hank," he jeered, and rolled away, laughing, as Hank threw a chunk of wood at him.

Jess got up and looked toward the wagon. He saw Dave coming in from the direction of the pass, a bedroll tucked under his arm and Maria at his heels. Surprise made a quick run through the big trail boss.

Luisa called out, her voice clear and alive and, for the first time since they had joined them, sounding happy.

"Coffee's ready — and breakfast in a few minutes!"

The Texans stowed away their bedrolls and moved toward the wagon, hungry now. They squatted around the fire, the coffee warming them, ridding them of the night's discomforts.

Jess saddled up and led his bay horse toward the fire. Dave, sipping coffee, looking surly, said, "I thought it over, Jess. I'm going to ride with you."

The big Texan's voice was short. "I'll do better alone." He poured himself some coffee, aware of Luisa watching. He said quietly, "The boys will give you a hand rounding up your sheep, Dave. Don't try to move them until I get back."

Anger darkened Dave's face. He put his cup down and stepped back from the fire, looking at Jess hunkered down across the blaze.

"You giving me orders now, Jess?"

A stillness fell across the watching men and fear flashed into Luisa's eyes. Urquillo, smoking his pipe, watched from beside the wagon, a frown on his face.

Jess' glance ran hard across the sheepman. He was suddenly aware of some streak of hostility in this man. It had been there all along, he thought, surfacing every now and then.

"They're my sheep," Dave said thinly. "It's my place to go."

"You tried it once before," Jess reminded him roughly. "We'll try it my way now!"

Dave shook his head. "Things have changed since then." His gaze slipped over the silent, watching Texans.

"They *have* to deal with me now!"

Jess frowned. "Deal?"

Dave licked his lips, his eyes guarded now, wary. "You know what I mean, Jess."

Jess said coldly, "No, I don't." He got to his feet, eyeing the sheepman. "I'm remembering you got us here on a lie, Dave. Maybe there's something else you haven't told us?"

The sheepman backed off a few paces, his eyes flinty. "I told you all you need to know. If you want to turn back now, I can't stop you . . ."

"We're not going back!" Jess cut in flatly. "But we're going into Paradise Valley my way — or we don't go in at all!"

It was an ultimatum and the big Texas trail boss meant it.

Dave's glance went to Urquillo, watching, silent . . . to Luisa. Shame appeared briefly on his dark features.

"All right," he said bitterly, "your way, Jess!" He threw his cup and stalked angrily away from the fire.

Jess watched him for a moment, brooding. Then his gaze went to his men, Randy in particular. "Keep an eye on him. I'll be back tonight."

Luisa came to him as he was about to mount. "Please . . . Jess." Her voice was soft, sad, too. "Dave wasn't always like this. He's been hurt . . . he's changed."

Jess nodded. "I'll remember that."

She watched him ride off, feeling suddenly desolate, lonely; the brightness was gone out of the morning.

And she was frightened.

Dave was unpredictable. But he was her brother, and she did not want to see him hurt.

XII

Sheriff Cal Tennelly came forward in his chair, his eyes narrow, blunting the surprise in him.

"You sure?"

Clay's grin was tight. "I'm sure. It's been more than five years, but even in the dark I couldn't mistake him. Jess Riley!"

Tennelly shook his head. He was a tall, rangy man, hard-muscled, standing more than six inches above Clay's five-eleven. He was a few years older. He had a slow way of talking, almost gentle. His faded blue eyes under a thatch of sandy hair added to what seemed a weak good nature: a man who would step aside at any real threat of trouble.

But the gun he wore high up at his waist, set for a cross draw, was not window dressing — and Hollister knew from past experience the innate ruthlessness of this man. Clay fancied himself pretty good with a hand gun, but he knew he couldn't match Tennelly; and he was aware few men in or out of Texas could.

"Riley — running with a sheepherder?" The sheriff settled back, a hard twist to his mouth. "Doesn't sound right, Clay."

Hollister shrugged. "Had some of his trail crew along . . . four or five, maybe. I couldn't see them too well."

He had had little sleep and he was tired, irritable. But he had come to Bentley because Tennelly had to know what had happened last night.

The sheriff got up and walked to the door. He looked outside, across the muddy street where he could make out a half-dozen buggies and wagons and some saddle horses tied up in front of the courthouse.

He watched this for a while, pondering the news Clay had brought him. When he turned there was a caution in his faded blue eyes.

"Kind of changes things, doesn't it, Clay —

Jess Riley throwing in with that sheepherder."

"Not for me!" Hollister said. A hard anger flickered in his eyes. "I wasn't expecting him last night . . . none of us were."

He crossed to the door and looked up the street. A sneer thinned the smile on his face. "Next time . . ."

"You're not good enough, Clay!" The sheriffs voice was blunt. "Stay away from Riley!"

Hollister's eyes turned sullen. "Maybe," he muttered and walked back into the office. He turned then, a glint in his eyes. "How about you, Cal? You've got a badge — you could make it legal."

Tennelly shrugged. "If it comes to that, Clay. . . ." His fingers went up to touch the old scar on his cheek.

"Then pin a badge on me!" Hollister growled. "Make things easier for us. I can easy get a dozen men to ride with me. We'll burn that sheep-herder out, Riley or no Riley!"

The sheriff shook his head. "We'll wait, Clay. See how the meeting comes out first."

"Wait?" Hollister was impatient. "I can tell you how that meeting will come out, Cal. That was Ned Sparrow's rider Jess shot up last night. He's ready to ride down the pass right now with his whole crew."

"What's holding him then?"

Hollister's eyes turned sullen. "Not my boss."

"John Hendrix?"

Hollister shrugged. "John and that Indian

84

agent, Poole. They don't want that kind of trouble."

Tennelly nodded. "That's why we've got to be careful. They carry a lot of weight in the Valley." He turned and looked back across the street, to the courthouse. "And I've got a feeling John Hendrix is getting suspicious."

"Of what?" Hollister's tone was skeptical. "He never paid any attention to Slip Jenkins' place before."

Tennelly smiled loosely. "The old man wasn't doing any rustling, either," he said dryly. He closed the door and walked back to his desk. "We need the Jenkins place, Clay. But one wrong move now and we lose it. That county clerk is skittish enough as it is."

"He's getting paid," Hollister said. "And no risk. All he has to do is change the county records!"

He walked to the window, scowling. They had a good thing going here and he didn't want to lose it. He turned to face the sheriff.

"We didn't figure on Riley," he said. "But it doesn't have to change things, Cal. Pin that badge on me. I won't be stopped this time!"

Tennelly eyed him, not yet convinced.

"There's only one way to stop that sheepman from coming in," Hollister snarled. "And you know what most of the valley cattlemen think of Riley joining up with him."

Tennelly nodded slowly. "There's a woman down there."

"She won't be hurt," Clay promised. "I don't want that kind of an investigation either."

Tennelly took a badge from his desk drawer and tossed it to Hollister.

"I don't care what happens to the others," he said coldly. "Just get Jess Riley and that sheepherder out of the way!"

He stood up and walked to the door. "I'm riding out to see Red tonight. Tell him and his boys to lay low for a while. I don't want any of John Hendrix's boys to start nosing around the Jenkins' place." He turned. "Officially I'll be out of town on business — law business. You understand? You'll be on your own tonight!"

Clay nodded. "Good enough!" He joined the sheriff at the door and opened it. "We'll make a clear sweep of it this time."

He stiffened and pulled back inside, his eyes flaring. Tennelly's glance shot out to the man riding slowly up the street toward them. He pushed Clay back and waited, his bulk blocking the doorway, the gun at his waist cold and deadly.

Jess Riley had come up along an old trail through Santiago Pass, wet and slippery after last night's rain. He rode up through dripping timber with the sound of rivulets gurgling, underlining a deep stillness and quiet, and then he was in the open and Paradise Valley lay before him, falling away to the north and east to desolate buttes and stony ridges.

It was a beautiful valley ringed by the Paradise Mountains on the west and south, ten miles wide and running more than twenty-five miles long before it funneled out into the badlands.

Rising in his stirrups the big Texan could see the chimney smoke from a ranch tucked in a fold in the hills, but closer and just off center in the valley the square blocks of a town caught his eye. He wanted to see John Hendrix, but he did not know this valley, and the ranch he saw in the distance could be anyone's; so Jess decided to ride on to Bentley first.

The sun rose and warmed the land and steam rose from the wet earth. Jess came across a wide stream rimmed by willows and running full. He followed it for several miles before the trail turned into a wider road and brought him into Bentley.

It was a middling town, he saw — a county seat mainly because much of this county was still sparsely populated. It had the usual number of saloons and businesses attendant on a cattle town, many of them attesting to the town's newness by the raw wood weathering slowly.

The courthouse, however, was more solidly built of stone and timbers, and seeing a number of wagons, buggies and horses parked in front of it Jess made his way toward it.

A heavily loaded wagon lumbering by cut off Jess's view of Tennelly in the doorway; he did not notice the lawman until he was by him and Tennelly's voice reached out to him, cool and waiting: "Jess!"

He swung around now and saw Tennelly. His gaze made a quick run over the man, seeing little change from the last time they had met, except for the badge on Tennelly's vest and the fact that he was standing under a sign that read: Sheriff's Office.

Jess said dryly, "Heard you were wearing a badge, Cal. Quite a change for you, isn't it?"

Tennelly took a cigar from his vest pocket and bit off an end. "No more than you, Jess." He spat shreds of tobacco from his mouth. "I hear you're running with sheepherders now?"

Jess' gaze went hard, remote. Someone moved in the office behind Tennelly but he could not make out who it was.

He said easily, "Hollister bring you the news?" and smiled thinly at the look in the sheriff's eyes.

"Figgered," Jess said. "You ran together back in Texas . . . no reason why it would change here."

Tennelly cupped a match to his cigar. His hands were steady.

"Hollister or any of the others," he said coldly. "Wouldn't make any difference."

He nodded toward the courthouse. "There's a bunch of angry cattlemen in there right now, holding a meeting. You know what they're talking about?"

Jess nodded. "Sheep."

"And a Texas traitor," Tennelly added.

"John Hendrix say that?" Jess murmured.

88

Tennelly shrugged. "Won't do you any good. Hendrix doesn't like sheep coming in here any more than the others."

"Maybe," Jess said. "Won't hurt to find out."

He swung his horse away from the law office and Tennelly drew his gun. "Jess," he said softly, and when the trail boss swung around in saddle, he added, "you're about as welcome in this valley as a polecat. If you're going into that meeting, there'll be trouble."

Jess lay his hands on his pommel, his eyes probing. "You stopping me, Cal?"

The rangy sheriff licked his lips. He had drawn on impulse and now he had to go through with it. Behind him he felt Hollister stir.

"Go ahead," he said. "But I want your gun!"

Jess pondered this, letting the silence run on between them.

"Hasn't been any trouble in the valley," Tennelly went on, "until you and that sheepherder showed up. I want to keep it that way."

He slipped his gun back into his holster, spreading his hands. "Fair enough, Jess?"

Jess eyed him for a long moment. "Fair enough." He took his gun out, handed it to the sheriff, then wheeled his bay around and headed for the courthouse.

Behind Tennelly, Hollister heaved a sigh of relief. The sheriff turned, his smile tight on his lips.

"We've got him," he said softly. "We've got Jess Riley."

XIII

The Paradise Valley cattlemen were in the small assembly hall of the courtroom, seated around a long table. There were more than a dozen men present, but only four of them really carried any weight:

Ned Sparrow, a small, wiry, peppery man with too many years of hard luck behind him, making him intolerant now, grasping and ruthless; beside him and joining forces with Sparrow, Lou Bretman, wifeless these past two years, turned sour — a bigger man physically than Sparrow, but content to follow along with him; John Hendrix, a spare, white-haired cattleman whose Circle H ranch was the biggest in the valley; and Lee Morgan, a quiet man in his early thirties with a worried look in his eyes and five small children depending on him. All were from Texas originally; none of them had been in Paradise Valley longer than five years; and all were really just getting settled, beginning to feel the effects of a few good years of raising beef behind them.

The others in the room were small farmers who ran a few head of cattle. They were dependent on the four big ranchers to stay in business. Except for one or two, most of them were afraid of, and hated, sheep. They liked the way things were in the valley and they were afraid of change.

They were listening to Ernest Poole, an Indian agent whose main responsibility concerned the Cheyenne reservation east of the valley. He was a small man with a job too big for him, an idealist in a time and place that had little regard for Indians or misplaced do-gooders.

". . . your fears are entirely unfounded, gentlemen. Studies have shown that sheep and cattle can get along quite well together . . ."

Sparrow interrupted him with a hoot. "Whose studies, Poole? Anybody ever ask Texans?"

Poole turned his watery gray eyes on the speaker. "Mister Sparrow, let me assure you . . ."

"Assure and be damned!" Sparrow snarled. He stood up, looking around at the others. "We gonna stay here an' let this easterner tell *us* how we should feel about sheep? Goddamn it, there's only one thing to do now. We all know what happens when sheep move onto a range. They drive cattle out! Is that what we've been sweating for here?"

Poole tried to interrupt, but Sparrow's voice rode over him. "I know what we should be doing . . . what we would have done, back in Texas. We'd be sending our riders down Santiago Pass to run that sheepherder out of here . . ."

Hendrix interrupted dryly, "Seems to me some of your men tried just that last night, Ned."

Sparrow turned his bitter glance on the white-haired cattleman. "They weren't looking for that kind of trouble, John." His voice was harsh. "Not from other Texans."

Bretman put in grimly, "What's stopping you, John? You stand to lose as much as any of us if Owens brings his sheep into the valley. Jenkins' spread borders on yours."

Hendrix nodded. "I don't like sheep . . . you know that, Ned. But killing a couple of sheep-herders, maybe even a woman . . ."

Sparrow said angrily, "Nobody's talking about killing women."

"Gentlemen . . . gentlemen. . . ." Poole's voice tried to rise above the angry voices. "Any sort of range war between sheepmen and cattlemen will only bring on a federal investigation."

But Sparrow was already striding toward him. He elbowed the Indian agent out of the way and faced the men around the long table.

"John," he said coldly, "I've got one of my best riders laid up with a bullet in him. Doc Lawson says Cantry will be lucky if he's out of bed in two or three weeks. And you're telling *me* to look out for a damned sheepherder!"

"I'm telling you!" The voice came from in back of those seated men, carrying over them to Sparrow.

Men turned and craned their necks to watch as Riley strode toward them. The big Texan's gaze ranged over them, trying to pick out men he might know . . . but they were strangers to him:

all except the spare, white-haired John Hendrix — and he had met Hendrix only once or twice at roundup time — and that had been all of seven years ago.

Sparrow eyed him with cold anger. "Who in hell are you?"

"Jess Riley," the trail boss said. "I'm the man who shot your rider."

Sparrow stiffened, his hand dropping to his holstered gun. Bretman said grimly, "You've got your nerve, coming here!"

"I came to avoid more trouble," Jess said.

"You goddamn traitor!" Sparrow snarled. He drew his gun and cocked it. "Get out of here, before I kill you."

Hendrix rose, putting his hand on Sparrow's arm. "None of that, Ned!" His tone was sharp. "Let him talk!"

"I've had enough of talk!" Sparrow said angrily. But he slid his gun back into his holster, his gaze bitter. John Hendrix carried a lot of weight in the valley.

Jess surveyed the hostile group. "Some of you may know me . . . most of you don't. Those who do, know I don't care for sheep any more than you do. But hating sheep is one thing — keeping a man off his land is another."

"What land?"

Jess fixed his gaze on Sparrow. "I saw Dave Owens's bill of sale . . . and his recorded deed."

"I don't care what you saw!" Sparrow growled. "That damned sheepherder tricked

Jenkins. Told him he was a cattleman." His fiery gaze took in the others. "We all know that deed ain't worth the paper it's written on!"

"I wouldn't say that, Ned!" Hendrix's voice was dry. "If that deed isn't worth anything, then ours aren't either."

Sparrow eyed the older man distrustfully; he resented John's security, his tolerance.

But his anger was directed at the big Texas trail boss. He shook his finger at him, rage thick in his voice: "Hell with you, Riley! Paper or no paper, that sheepman ain't coming in here!"

Bretman stood up alongside Sparrow. "That's the way I feel, too." His lips curled contemptuously as he ran his gaze up and down Riley's big frame. "You'd risk your neck for a sheepman, Riley?"

Riley nodded coldly.

Hendrix frowned. "Why, Jess? What's this sheepherder to you?"

"He gave me a hand when I needed it," Jess said evenly. "I promised I'd help him get his sheep into Paradise Valley." His gaze lay hard on Bretman and Sparrow. "I don't care either way about sheep. But the way I figger it, a man has a right to his land — or none of us have!"

Sparrow's voice was tight: "Then you're coming in?"

Jess nodded. "Just for the record, there's six of us, backing Owens!" He let the silence run between them, and then added bluntly, "We're not looking for trouble. But it's your choice, gentlemen!"

He saw Sparrow's eyes flicker then, and Hendrix turn slightly and frown. Something warned him then and he started to turn, only to stop as something hard jammed none too gently against the small of his back.

"You've got trouble, Riley," the voice behind him said, and turning Jess saw Tennelly step back a pace, his gun cocked and ready. Behind him, in the doorway, Hollister waited, a rifle in his hands.

Tennelly said coolly, "You're under arrest, Riley."

The big Texan's gaze slid to Hollister and held briefly on the badge pinned to Hollister's shirt. Something dark and angry twisted through Jess then, knowing he had been tricked and he had been a party to it.

But he held his voice cold and even: "What for? This was an open meeting."

"Attempted murder," Tennelly said. "Hollister swore out a warrant. Shooting Les Cantry last night, without provocation."

Jess looked contemptuously at Hollister, then at Sparrow. "Is that what your rider told you?"

Sparrow's eyes glittered. "Cantry was in no condition to do much talking," he said. "But Clay was there. If he says you shot my rider . . ."

"He's a liar!" Jess said bleakly.

"I've got four witnesses," Hollister said. "Cantry was in his saddle, arguing with that

95

sheepman friend of yours when you shot him."

Jess started for him, but Tennelly blocked his way. "You'll have a chance to tell your story in court, Riley!" He nodded toward the door. "Let's go!"

Jess turned to Hendrix. "It's a frame, John . . . you know it . . . and the rest of you do, too."

John said quietly, "Maybe, Jess. But keeping you in jail for a few days won't hurt — and it might help cool things down."

Jess studied him for a long moment, his lips thinning. "A fair shake, John," he said softly. "One Texan to another. That's what I expected . . ."

Bretman cut in: "You got your fair shake, Riley! You're lucky it's jail, instead of a hanging!"

Tennelly shoved him toward the door, his grin cold and malicious. "Might still be a hanging, if that sheepman friend of yours tries to shoot his way into the valley!"

XIV

Luisa came away from the stream, carrying a bucket of water. Pausing by the wagon to look toward the cut of Santiago Pass, the memory of the big Texan who had ridden off occupied her thoughts. Until Jess returned she would not rest easy.

Her brother, Urquillo and Riley's men were

96

off, rounding up the scattered sheep. She was alone here, with the wagon and the chores, and a longing rose sharply in her to be rid of this endless journeying.

She would tell Jess, when he returned, she thought — tell him that Dave was her brother, not her husband, and that Urquillo was their father. It was not fair to her or to Jess, this lie. Everything in her cried out against this.

Baldo's whine brought her attention to the box under the wagon where the sheep dog lay. She smiled sadly and knelt in front of him, pouring some water in a dish for him. He lapped at it, his big eyes fixed on her.

"You'll be fine," she said, and then turned as she heard the rider.

Dave Owens dismounted a few feet away and strode toward her. He looked more gaunt these days, she thought, and grim.

He knelt beside her and ran his fingers gently over the dog's head, scratching him affectionately behind the ears. Baldo whined softly and licked his hand.

"Easy, boy," Dave said softly. "She'll be working the sheep together in another week or so."

Watching him Luisa felt a shadow fall across her soul. He was a man of violent emotions, her brother, gentle with the dogs, hard with her, rebellious and angry with his father.

She had known him when he was different; and she would always remember the day he had come home from school, his nose bleeding, a cut over his right eye. He hadn't cried. She could not remember ever having seen her brother cry.

"Damned greaser!" That's what they had called him and he had looked at his father and mother, his eyes laying them open, asking a question they could not answer. "Why?"

He had changed from that day. He was no longer Antonio, the dark-haired, smiling boy who had teased his younger sister and brought flowers home to his mother.

He spent most of his time studying the Anglos in town, imitating the riders he saw, the way they dressed and the way they walked. He worked on his speech, too, hardening the liquid sound of his voice, making it more slurred, drawling, and faintly arrogant. And he worked hardest with his pistol, learning to draw, to shoot; over this had begun his alienation with his father.

It came to a head, finally: The widening gulf between Texas cattlemen and sheepmen. Drought was more to blame, perhaps, than sheep; but withered grass and closecropping sheep had fanned frustration into hatred.

Urquillo had stopped Antonio the night the riders came and told them to leave. Her brother would have been killed if he hadn't. They made Urquillo a fair offer for his place and let him keep his sheep.

"Just move on," they told him, and it was plain that this offer would not hold long.

She was thinking this, feeling again a great

sadness, when Dave straightened and went to his bedroll, taking from a small canvas bag, where he kept among his personal items, a box of shells. He slipped this into his pocket as he walked back to his horse.

"Antonio," she said, fear in her heart. "Where are you going?"

He turned on her, his voice short: "Paradise Valley."

She came to him now, putting a hand quickly on his arm. "No . . . no. Jess said to wait."

He shoved her hand away. "Jess?" There was a sneer in his voice. "Is that what he is to you?"

She said stiffly, "Antonio . . ."

But he cut her off. "What is there between you?"

She reacted to the harshness in his face. All her life she had backed off from her brother and her father.

"I'm in love with him," she answered.

He laughed mockingly. "And him?"

She faltered. "I . . . I don't know."

"I saw the way he looked at you last night," Dave said. "If he. . . ." He paused and then added, "I'll kill him first!"

"Kill?" She stepped back from him, anger flaring in her. "He's done nothing except to risk his life for you." She flung an arm in the direction of the pass. "Right now he's in Paradise Valley, trying to . . ."

"Do what?" Dave asked. She stared at him. "How do we know what he's doing? He's a

Texan. He may be selling us out for all I know."

She shook her head. "Antonio . . . how can you say that?"

"Well," he said, overriding her, "I'm going to beat him to it. It took a bit of doing, but I got Riley and his men here. Texans against Texans. The way I planned it."

"Planned it?"

He looked off; they were alone. His smile was cold. "Jess thinks I saved his life. He doesn't know I waited until I saw him coming. I poisoned that water hole, Luisa. Then I waited."

She backed away from him until the wagon stopped her; her hands fell limply by her sides.

"Antonio . . ." she whispered.

"Don't look so shocked!" he said harshly. "They ran us out of our home, didn't they? Texans! Now . . ." his voice turned soft and wicked, "now it's my turn."

He mounted and started to turn away; he looked back, his eyes bitter, his voice cutting at her. "You're a fool, Luisa. Falling in love with him. You — a *greaser!*"

Her hand came up to her mouth, her eyes brimming with unshed tears. He laughed softly.

"I used him, Luisa. And after today I won't need Jess any more — or any of them."

He whirled away then, sending his pony pounding up the trail toward Paradise Valley.

She remained for long moments by the wagon, numbed by the savagery in her brother's face, torn apart by his words.

"No . . ." she whispered softly. "Not . . . Jess. . . ."

But she was not sure and that hurt most of all.

Randy Williams glanced up at the sun. It was mid-afternoon and getting warm again. He chased a lamb out of a draw and watched it run toward the flock growing on that flat below.

Urquillo and Maria were working the thickets further south; Randy could hear the sheep dog's barking. The others were scattered along the foothills, doing what he was doing.

Randy wiped sweat from his brow with the back of his sleeve. He still didn't like working sheep, and he felt irritated and faintly resentful that Jess had not allowed him to ride along to Paradise Valley.

Hank drifted over, his steerhorn mustache drooping. He glanced off where Larry was working, closer to the pass.

"See Dave around?"

Randy shook his head. "He was working east of me, with the old man, last time I saw him." He paused. "Funny thing about Dave."

"Now don't get on that horn again," Hank grumbled.

"Hell," Randy snapped, and started to turn away. Then he swiveled around again, frowning. "Why'd you ask?"

"Thought I saw him head back to the wagon."

Randy scratched his head. "Dave's been acting strange since Jess left. Reckon he didn't like being put down the way he was."

Chuck and Bob Rich joined them. "Reckon that's about all of them," Chuck said. He shook his head, grinning. "Getting so I'm beginning to feel for the poor dumb critters."

Rich smiled. "Getting used to the smell, too." He put his gaze on Hank. "You look worried."

Hank ran his fingers through his mustache. "Hope Jess manages to talk some sense into those Paradise Valley ranchers." He looked at Randy. "When'ud he say he'd be back?"

The red-headed *segundo* shrugged. "Don't remember if he said. But if he ain't back by suppertime. . . ."

Larry rode up. "Looks like a conference." He grinned. "Whatever it is, count me in."

Randy said, "Hell, I'm hungry. Let's go back, give Dave's wife a hand. I want to have a pow-wow with Dave anyway."

Luisa was still standing by the wagon when they rode up. She had been crying.

Randy said, not noticing at first: "Where's your husband, ma'am?"

She didn't answer him.

Randy frowned. "Larry said he thought he saw Dave riding up the pass a few minutes ago?"

She nodded numbly.

Randy glanced quickly at his companions. "Where did he go, Mrs. Owens?"

"Paradise Valley." She sagged against the wagon. "And . . . he isn't my husband."

They stared at her.

"He's my brother. He said he was riding into the valley to make a deal."

Randy stiffened, all his old suspicions coming alive again.

"What kind of a deal?"

"I don't know," she said. Then, turning away, the tears coming again: "Please . . ." she said, and went inside the wagon.

Randy eyed the pass. The sun was low, slanting shadows across the foothills.

"I don't know what's going on," he said grimly, "But I'm riding up after Jess."

"Hell!" Larry said sharply, "we'll all go."

Randy shook his head. "Someone has to stay here . . . keep an eye on that . . . that girl. And the sheep. We can't just up and leave them."

He slid his hand down over his holstered Colt. "If Jess is on the way back, I'll run into him. If he ain't. . . ."

He whirled his horse around and rode off.

XV

Dave Owens topped the pass and swung off the trail now, keeping to the brush. He had been here before and he knew where he was going. He had come this far riding easy, his only worry that he might run into Jess coming back; from here on the odds were greater that he would run into hostile riders if he stuck to the valley roads.

Off in the distance, against the darkening

plain, he saw the splotch that was Bentley. Closer, tucked away in a fold in the hills, he could make out the tiny buildings of Ned Sparrow's spread.

North of this lay the ranch he had bought in good faith, hidden beyond the timbered ridges that slanted off toward the badlands. Just this side of it was John Hendrix's place, and that was where he was headed.

He rode warily, keeping to the timber. The sun went down, its rays dying against the clouds that drifted like white gull feathers on the horizon. He stopped once, listening, as riders came by on the trail below. They faded off toward Bentley.

He had half expected to run into Jess, and now the thought came to him that something might have happened to the big trail boss. He had said what he said to his sister out of some dark and inner malice. He knew Jess was not selling them out; he had come to know the big Texan well enough to be sure of this.

If something had happened to Jess it would weaken his hand and leave his sister and father with two less men to defend them. He thought of this and cursed Jess; but he had planned this too long and now he had to see it through.

The land sloped toward the north and the day died, the shadows crawling down from the hills. Dave had to chance the road now; he was not familiar enough with the valley to find his way to John Hendrix's ranch in the dark.

He stayed between the wagon ruts until the lights of the main building broke the night's blackness on his right. A few hundred yards beyond he came upon the turnoff to the Hendrix ranch.

He pulled aside now and considered his next move, his lips thinning at what he might encounter, his hand sliding down across the comforting feel of his gunbutt.

Hendrix's ranch hands wouldn't be expecting him. A bluff should see him through.

He let his horse drift slowly now, a cool rising wind at his back. It was a quarter of a mile in to the ranch yard. Tall trees lined the road, and he was grateful for the shadows.

Eventually he rode past a corral and the looming shadow of a windmill, well greased and spinning almost noiselessly, pumping water up into a big tank balanced on iron stilts. Voices drifted out to him from the long galley and then, as he came into the yard, a man moved out of the shadows by the bunkhouse and hailed sharply, "Hold it, mister!" Dave pulled aside and waited.

A lanky man moved up and stopped as he recognized Dave in the paleness just beyond the light from the ranchhouse. He said, "The sheepman," and then hard and without humor: "Say one thing for you, fella, you got a helluva nerve!"

Dave said, "I've come to see John Hendrix."

The lanky man called to another just coming out of the galley and the man drifted out toward the house. He returned a few minutes later with the foreman, a rangy, craggy-faced man named Jedman.

Jedman said, "You want to see Mr. Hendrix?" At Dave's nod: "What about?"

"Sheep," Dave said with faint insolence. "And . . . a deal."

Jedman eyed him in the dark, a coolness and a faint admiration in his eyes.

"I'm a neighbor," Dave went on. "Whether you like it or not. My place is just north of here. That's what I want to talk to Mr. Hendrix about."

Jedman nodded. "I'll see if he'll talk to you," he said. He turned to the lanky man. "Keep an eye on him, Pete."

A few moments later John Hendrix came out to the broad, covered veranda with his foreman. He eyed Dave for a long moment, his eyes sombre. Then he said abruptly, "Come inside."

Dave dismounted and followed the rancher into a big, comfortably furnished living room. There was a small fire flickering in the fireplace and a china-based lamp on a small table by a desk. Hendrix's wife, a slender, cheerful woman with hair as white as her husband's, looked in on them, a small anxiety in her eyes.

John said, "It's all right, Nora." When she withdrew he turned to Dave. "Drink? I've got ten-year whiskey in the cupboard."

Dave shook his head. "Never learned to like the stuff."

Hendrix shrugged. "Just as well." He poured

himself a drink and sank down into a comfortable chair across from Dave.

"All right," he said quietly. "What do you want to talk about?"

"Fifteen thousand dollars," Dave replied. "In cash."

Hendrix jerked forward, his eyes cold. "For what?"

Dave smiled coolly. "Call it nuisance value, Mr. Hendrix. You pay me fifteen thousand dollars and I don't come into the Valley with my sheep." He settled back, watching the old rancher. "You can even have the Jenkins place."

Hendrix said evenly, "Your price is too high, Mr. Owens. That rundown spread isn't worth more than four thousand and I don't believe you paid more."

"Call the rest of it damages," Dave said. "My pride, Mr. Hendrix." He made a small tent of his fingers on his lap, but Hendrix was suddenly aware of the gun jutting from Dave's holster and a small surprise went through him.

Hendrix shook his head. "You've come to the wrong man, Mr. Owens."

"I've got six men behind me," Dave interrupted coldly. "Texans . . . like yourself. And Jess Riley."

"Riley's in jail," Hendrix said brusquely. "In Bentley."

A small shock went through the sheepman and his eyes narrowed in momentary confusion. *Damn him,* he thought, and then he smiled.

"Jess's friends won't like that," he said. "If Paradise Valley wants trouble, this is the way to get it."

Hendrix got up and placed his empty glass on the small table.

Dave said easily, "Last night some riders from the valley tried to burn me out. One of them was shot. They could try again." He stood up. "I'm thinking of my wife, Mr. Hendrix. I don't want her hurt. But I'm not giving up the Jenkins place, just because some of the cattlemen here hate sheep." He paused, eyeing the white-haired man. "Fifteen thousand dollars, Mr. Hendrix — and there won't be any trouble. Cheap enough, I'd say."

Hendrix frowned, but he was considering it. It was a stiff price to pay, but it would save bloodshed. And Hendrix had seen too many range wars in the past; no one ever won.

"What about Jess?" he asked.

Dave shrugged, a glint in his eyes. "He came along to help me. Why should he balk now?"

Hendrix plucked at his chin. "All right," he said finally. "I'll talk to Lou Bretman and Ned Sparrow."

"Talk isn't enough," Dave said smoothly.

Hendrix turned on him, his voice irritable. "What do you want then?"

Dave hesitated. "Your word. That'll be enough for me."

Hendrix studied him for a moment, then nodded. "I'll have the money for you tomorrow.

Some time in the afternoon."

Dave smiled. He had expected more opposition. He said, "Tomorrow, then."

Hendrix walked to the door with him.

"All right, Pete," he said to the man holding Dave's horse.

Dave mounted, backing off a bit. He raised his hand to Hendrix on the porch, then whirled and rode rapidly out of the ranchyard.

Jedman came out of the shadows to join Hendrix. "What did he want, John?"

The old cattleman was staring off into the night. "Saddle a couple of horses," he said quietly. "We're going calling on Ned Sparrow and Lou Bretman."

XVI

Jess Riley paced inside his cell, a wildness in his eyes. He saw the day fade against the barred window of his cell and his thoughts went to Luisa waiting for him at the mouth of Santiago Pass.

A wind began blowing steadily outside, rattling loose boards, sending a vagrant can tumbling down the street. He turned and sat down on the edge of his bunk, a bleak anger making a cold hard knot in the pit of his stomach.

He had come to Paradise Valley in good faith, but he saw now that words were useless. John Hendrix was neutral, but he would not help; Bretman and Ned Sparrow were too blinded by their hatred and fear of sheep to think rationally.

Hollister had lied and they chose to believe him. Jess knew that Hollister couldn't make it stick in court, but he had a feeling neither Hollister nor Tennelly really cared. They had wanted Jess out of the way, and this had provided them with convenient means.

What for?

Hollister and Tennelly had been thick as thieves back in Texas, and Jess knew that a man like Tennelly didn't change just because he put on a badge.

He got up and walked to the cell door as Tennelly came back, followed by a shuffling, slack-jawed, balding man.

Tennelly slanted a look at the big Texan, then went on and dropped some old newspapers and a copy of the Police Gazette on the desk. A picture of a buxom girl in scanty attire took up most of the front page under a blaring headline. CURVACEOUS CUTIE FOUND IN SOCIALITE'S BED.

"This oughta keep you awake tonight, Virg," he said, grinning. And then, putting his cold glance on Jess, he added, "I want to see him still in there when I get back!"

Virgil Holmes shrugged. "He'll be there."

He was a part time deputy, an odd-jobs man who worked just enough to keep him in whiskey. He had a wasted frame and furrowed cheeks, but he knew how to handle a gun. He had worked as a top wrangler for a big cattle outfit before a bronc had put him out of commission. He still walked with a slight limp.

He went over to the desk, settled himself in Tennelly's chair and glanced disinterestedly at the Police Gazette.

"How long you figgerin' to be gone?" he asked Tennelly.

"Should be back before sundown tomorrow," Cal said. He took a brush jacket from a hook. "Law says we have to feed him . . . see that he gets breakfast, but have it brought in here. I don't want you out of sight of him at any time."

Virgil crossed his rundown boots on Tennelly's desk and picked up the Police Gazette.

"Looks like it's gonna be a long dry spell," he grumbled.

"There's half a bottle of whiskey in the drawer," Tennelly said. "Make it last."

Virgil glanced at Jess. "He got any friends?"

"Not in town," Tennelly said. He smiled loosely. "If he gives you trouble, put a bullet in him. Won't be anybody in the valley who'll blame you."

He started for the door.

Jess said, "Kind of late to go riding, Tennelly?"

The sheriff looked back at him. "Ain't it," he said tonelessly, and went out.

Virgil got up and went to the door and bolted it. Then he went back to the desk, pulled out a drawer and found the whiskey. He settled back in the chair and tilted the bottle to his lips.

Jess said, "Where's the sheriff going?"

Virgil ignored him.

The Texas trail boss took a new tack. "Hey, it's getting cold in here. How about a drink?"

Virgil slipped his Colt out and placed it on the desk beside him. He said dispassionately, "Mister, you talk too much . . . gets me nervous." He turned his gaze on Jess, his lips going slack, ugly. "Might make me just nervous enough for you to have an accident."

Dave Owens was riding back toward Santiago Pass, an elation singing in him. He had humbled the Paradise Valley cattlemen and blackmailed them into giving him fifteen thousand dollars. That was what he had wanted, why he had tricked the Texas trail boss and his men into backing him.

Luisa wouldn't understand; neither would his father. The old rebellion flared up in him. His father was a fool, living out of his time. He was a sheepman in a country that hated sheep, and in some quarters looked upon as a foreigner and despised.

But he and Luisa had been born in Texas, and his father had made his home there. The injustice of this burned like gall in Dave and would never die.

He pulled off the trail now, not wanting to risk running into riders from other ranches. He topped a small rise and dismounted, giving his horse a breather. In the distance he saw the lights of Bentley against the flat darkness of Paradise Valley.

He thought of Riley then, and a sneer crowded out any concern he might have felt for the man. Riley was a fool and had brought his predicament upon himself. And anyway, he didn't need the big Texan now.

He was about to mount again when he heard a rider. His horse moved restlessly and Dave clamped his fingers over the horse's muzzle, stilling him.

The rider passed just below him, moving at a good clip, heading north. There was a wind blowing from the north, rustling dead leaves and moving branches; but the rider came by too close for Dave not to recognize him.

Cal Tennelly!

The sheriff was headed north, and curiosity stirred in Dave. Tennelly could be going to see John Hendrix, but the sheepman didn't think so. There was something about the way Tennelly was riding, with a slicker roll tied to his cantle, that indicated he was headed somewhere for a longer stay.

The ranch he had bought lay in that direction, and now a brightness crept into the sheepman's eyes.

He mounted and swung around, following the sheriff now lost in the night's blackness. The wind was blowing in his face and he knew Tennelly couldn't hear him. Up ahead hoofbeats drummed faintly against the night.

He came finally upon the cutoff road that led to John Hendrix's ranch. He could see the lights of the place off to his right, but Tennelly had not gone there.

Tennelly was still moving north. Dave knew now that Tennelly was headed for the Jenkins place, or some rendezvous in the badlands beyond.

He hesitated. It was none of his business what the sheriff did; but then, remembering the way Tennelly had humiliated him, driving him out of Paradise Valley, a hard and bitter light came into the sheepman's eyes. His hand slipped down over his Colt and he let it lay there as he followed.

Beyond Hendrix's spread the road climbed for a mile or two then began to drop off, curving toward the long sheer bulk of a sparsely timbered ridge. The Jenkins place lay here, backed up against the ridge. The road ended here, too, for beyond the ridge lay the broken buttes and eroded gullies of the badlands where no honest riders rode.

The wind was whistling now out of the badlands, with enough chill to it to give it an edge. Dave rode slowly, listening to the rider ahead. The urgency had gone out of the hoofbeats.

Up ahead now Dave could see the spread he had bought: a small but sturdy house of split logs, chinked and windproofed, a corral, empty now, although Dave thought he saw a horse move in the shadows at the far end. There were several small outbuildings, and a natural spring flowing from the base of the ridge provided plenty of water.

It was everything he had told Luisa and his father — a good place to settle down, run sheep — but the thought brought only anger and no sense of regret.

He eased his mount to a stop and watched as Tennelly came out of the deep shadows and rode directly toward the house. Dave's hand went to his rifle and he drew it slowly from its scabbard. He saw Tennelly pull up in front of the house and wait as the door creaked open and a thick shape appeared against the blackness inside. Light glinted faintly from a gun muzzle.

The sheriff said, "Red . . . Tennelly!"

The broad figure moved out of the doorway toward the sheriff. He was still holding his gun, but loosely now. He glanced off into the night behind Tennelly.

"You alone?"

Tennelly nodded. "Where're the boys?"

"Back at the hideout," Red answered. "We just finished rebranding."

Tennelly said, "Move them in the morning, Red. Get them out of there."

Red said easily, "What's the hurry? We were figgerin' to pick up another dozen head of John Hendrix stock before . . ."

"Not now!" Tennelly's voice was irritable. "Wait until things blow over."

"The sheepman?"

Tennelly nodded. "Hollister is taking care of him tonight!" He rubbed his cold hands together. "Old friend of ours showed up, Red — Jess Riley!"

The blocky man stiffened. "What's he doing here?"

"Joined up with that sheepman," Tennelly answered.

Watching from up the trail Dave's fingers tightened on his rifle. But the distance was too far, and a miss would put him in trouble. Reluctantly he slipped the rifle back into its holster.

Rustlers! That must have been the trouble old man Jenkins had hinted at.

Hell with it, Dave thought. Why should he care if these men stole the valley ranches blind?

Below him Tennelly's hard voice rode the cold wind. "That's why I want you to move the cows we've got now. And keep clear of this place. Hendrix is getting suspicious."

"I know," the blocky man said. "I've been seeing some of his riders lately up this way."

He started to turn into the corral, stopped . . . and stepped back swiftly, his gun coming up, his eyes probing the shadows uptrail.

"Hear anything?" he rasped.

Tennelly looked back but saw nothing. He shook his head.

"Thought I heard a horse whinny," Red said. He stood there, still watching, not sure.

"Probably yours," Tennelly said. "Come on,

116

I'm riding with you."

Red went into the corral and brought out his horse. It was already saddled. He and Tennelly rode away together, moving toward the broken dark land beyond.

Dave was standing by his mount, his fingers clamped on his horse's nostrils. He waited until the sound of their passage faded against the night, then mounted, whirling sharply.

He was thinking of what Tennelly had said about Hollister going down the Pass again, tonight. He was thinking of his father, and Luisa.

His horse slipped on a rock and the animal stumbled. He jerked on his reins, the bit biting cruelly into the animal's mouth. "Come on, dammit," he snarled.

But the mare limped badly, whinnying with hurt sound.

Dave dismounted and ran his fingers down the animal's left forefoot. Something warm and sticky clung to his fingers.

He straightened slowly, looking off. It was going to be a long hard walk back down the pass.

XVII

Randy Williams spotted the lights of Bentley as he dipped down into Paradise Valley. An hour later he was riding down the town's main street, bucking a cold wind that sent most of Bentley's inhabitants indoors. Those who were about gave the redheaded Texan only a cursory glance. No one knew him here, Randy reflected, except Tennelly, and he kept a wary eye out for the lawman as he rode slowly, slouched in the saddle, past the law office.

He drifted against the wind, looking for a saloon. If something had happened to Jess that was the most likely place in which to find out.

A tinny piano and whiskey-thickened voices drew him toward a building which a sign creaking in the wind labeled: CIMMARON BAR. Randy tied up at the crowded rail and went inside.

A bad oil painting of the Cimmaron River with wildeyed steers crossing it hung behind the bar. Several girls in short skirts and painted faces sat and laughed with customers at nearby tables.

Randy cruised toward the bar and found a place next to a huge man nursing a beer between gnarled hands.

"Shot of Texas redeye," he said as the bartender approached him. He rubbed his hands together. "Feels like a Panhandle norther blowing out there tonight."

The bartender grinned. He had a red brush mustache under a generous nose, a ruddy, ageless sort of face and an expansive attitude toward life. He had been born with another name, but here he was known as Cimmaron and unless legally required, Cimmaron was what he answered to.

He poured Randy a shot. "This'll curl your toes, stranger."

Randy eyed the amber liquor in his glass. "Hope so," he grinned. "Though I ain't seen nothing that compares with the redeye they serve a man in Holtsville on the Brazos."

The bartender said affably, "Texan?"

Randy nodded. "Drifting through . . . heading north." He downed the drink, gasped, and shook his head slowly as he set the empty glass down on the bar.

"Now that's redeye," he said. He pushed the glass toward the bartender. "One more oughta do it, mister . . ."

"Cimmaron," the bartender said. "I own the place." He started to pour, paused . . . then sniffed the air and frowned.

"Hey, Josh — you smell something?"

The big man with the beer turned his head, wrinkling his nose. "Thought it was only me." He looked at Randy. "If I didn't know better I'd say it was sheep."

Randy put a cold level gaze on the man. "Where I come from, mister, that's a dirty word!"

Josh shrugged. "Same here." But he wrinkled his nose, scowling. "You come through that sheep camp at the head of the pass?"

Randy feigned innocence. "What sheep camp?"

Cimmaron answered. "Some damn fool with a flock of sheep is trying to settle in the valley. Got

119

the whole place stirred up . . . the cattlemen, anyway."

Randy frowned. "Can't say I blame them. Sheep, eh? Holy hell!" He drained his glass, took a deep breath, and shoved the empty back toward Cimmaron. "One more, for the road."

The bartender obeyed. "Damned if that sheep smell ain't getting worse."

He turned to some men at a nearby table. "Hey, Nick . . . come here a minit."

The pock-faced man turned his head toward the bar and Randy tensed, recognizing him as one of the riders who had visited the sheep camp with Hollister last night.

Nick said grouchily, "What in hell you want?"

Cimmaron cut him off, waving impatiently. "Just come here a minit. Nick."

Nick scowled, but threw in his cards and stood up. It was a bad hand anyway and he was not too displeased at the interruption.

"Stand right there," the bartender instructed as Nick came up. Then, as Nick paused: "Smell anything?"

"Cripes!" Nick exploded angrily. "You mean yuh called me up here to —" He stopped, sniffing the air. "Smells like . . . like sheep dip."

Cimmaron nodded. "Figgered you'd know."

Nick eyed Randy through narrow, suspicious eyes. "Was a bunch of renegade Texans down at that sheep camp, mister. Mebbe you're one of them?"

Randy's hand came up with a gun in it and Nick stiffened.

"Where I come from," Randy said coldly, "we kill men who say things like that!"

Nick licked his lips. He wasn't sure, but Randy could have been one of the men he saw last night.

"You talk big," he said thinly, "with a gun in your hand."

Randy was running a bluff and he knew he had to see it through. He put his gun on the counter, pushed it toward Cimmaron, and turned just in time to meet Nick's rush.

Nick drove him back against the bar and Randy wrestled him around, jammed his forearm into his face and then slammed two quick punches to the man's middle. Nick doubled and Randy's right sent him caroming into the poker table he had left. Men scattered as he fell across the table, then twisted to his feet. His hand started to drop to his gun, but stopped as Cimmaron laid the twin barrels of his shotgun across the bar.

"It was a fair fight, Nick," the bartender said coldly.

He waited until Nick calmed down and settled back in the poker game before putting the shotgun away. He shoved Randy's gun back to him and the Texan holstered it, touching the bruise on his jaw.

Cimmaron said, "From the looks of you it ain't the first fight you been in lately, mister."

Randy shrugged.

"Staying in town?" Cimmaron asked. It was an idle question without much interest.

"Only tonight," Randy said. Then grinned. "Too much talk of sheep bothers me."

Josh finished his beer and looked at Randy. "Bothers all of us," he said. " 'Specially the sheriff." He shoved his glass to Cimmaron for a refill. "Look out for him, mister. He's just jailed a Texas trail boss name of Riley."

Cimmaron was refilling Josh's glass. "Know him?"

Randy shook his head. "Heard of him." He glanced at Nick but the cowboy was studying his cards and seemed to have lost interest in Randy.

"What'd Riley do? Smell of sheep?"

"Worse. He's thrown in with that sheepman camped down at the mouth of the pass."

Randy shook his head. "A Texan — running with a sheepman?" He shoved a silver dollar on the counter. "Where's the best place in town to bunk out . . . some place that's quiet and without bedbugs in the mattress?"

"Try the Stockman's Hotel," Cimmaron said. "If you were staying a while I'd say Ma Shaughnessy's boarding house."

Randy nodded. "I'll try the hotel."

Cimmaron and Josh both watched him leave. Josh frowned. "You still smell it?" he asked the bartender.

Cimmaron sniffed the air. "Yeah . . . a little." Then he shrugged. "Hell, Josh, maybe it's just our imagination . . . what with all this talk about sheep in the valley.

Jess Riley lay on his back on the bunk, staring up at the ceiling. Inside the office Virgil Holmes was searching the place for more whiskey. Jess could hear him curse softly as he opened and slammed shut drawers and cupboards.

There was a knock on the door. Jess heard it above the noise of the wind outside and he turned to look toward the office. Virgil was too intent on what he was doing and seemed not to have heard.

He walked back to the desk, picked up the empty whiskey bottle the sheriff had left him, drained the last few drops and slammed it into the waste basket.

The knock on the door was louder.

Virgil eyed it, frowning. Tennelly had been explicit: *let nobody in!* And Tennelly was not a man to cross.

"Who is it?"

"Supper for the prisoner," the man outside said.

Jess came up to sit on the edge of his bunk. He had recognized Randy's voice.

Virgil considered this. Tennelly had mentioned breakfast, not supper.

"He's already had his supper," he said.

There was a moment's silence, then the man outside said, "Must be a mistake then. Restaurant down the street said to bring him a tray."

Virgil crossed to the window and looked outside. He could just make out a shadowy figure standing in front of the door, holding what looked like a covered tray.

"I got orders to let no one inside," he said.

The shadowy figure shrugged. "Hell, I don't care. Hate to see this food go to waste, though. I even brung a bottle along . . . thought the sheriff was in and might like a nip on a cold night."

Virgil licked his lips. "Whiskey?"

"Cimmaron's best. Well, sorry, fella." The man outside started to turn away.

Virgil said sharply, "Hold on there, mister!"

He went to the door, slipped the bolt back and dropped his hand to his gun.

"No sense in wasting it," he agreed. "Just pass the bottle . . . I'll see the sheriff gets it."

"Sure," the man said.

Virgil opened the door a crack. The man outside slammed his shoulder against it, sending the jailer reeling back. Before he could recover and draw his gun Randy was in the room, palming his Colt. He slammed the barrel across Virgil's head and the man slumped to the floor.

Jess was at the cell door. "The keys are hanging on the wall, by the desk," he told Randy.

The redheaded segundo gave him a quick grin as he opened the cell. Jess went immediately to the desk, took his gun from the drawer where Tennelly had placed it and slid it into his holster.

Randy was dragging Virgil's unconscious body into the cell; Jess gave him a hand.

He eyed the lump under Randy's eye. "Fighting again?"

Randy said laconically, "Yeah."

He motioned to the door. "I got your bay saddled and waiting across the street with mine." He grinned. "The stableman put up a fuss . . . I had to quiet him a little."

They crossed the street and got into saddle with no one noticing. The wind was in their face as they rode quickly out of town, heading for the pass.

XVIII

Luisa lay huddled by the fire-gutted wagon, numbed and vacant-eyed, her hands fumbling aimlessly among the contents of her charred, hidebound chest. A few feet away Urquillo lay, his back propped against a wheel. He had taken a bullet in his side. A bandage stemmed the slow flow of blood. He lay there quietly, his eyes dark, staring off into the night. His shotgun lay at his side.

A small campfire cast a flickering glow of light just beyond; but the wind sliding down through the pass was cold, beating against the branches of the trees along the creek.

Maria crept out from under the wagon to stand beside her. The sheep dog looked off into the darkness and whined. Luisa didn't move. Maria barked sharply now and bristled. Urquillo stirred, his hand reaching for his shotgun.

Luisa roused now. She stared toward the oncoming riders, a fear in her eyes; then, as the riders came full into the firelight she came to her feet, a sob of relief clutching at her throat.

"Jess . . . Jess. . . ."

The big Texas trail boss dismounted and went to her, sweeping her into his arms. She clung to him, crying softly, repeating, "Jess . . . oh, Jess. . . ."

He held her tightly, his face grim as he surveyed the scene. The wagon was burned down to its bed, but it could still roll. The smell of charred wood and burned cloth lingered on the cold air.

Behind Jess, still mounted, Randy swore.

Jess glanced at Urquillo. "How is he, Luisa?"

The girl looked up into Jess' grim face, then at her father. She said brokenly, "He's hurt . . . not badly."

"And . . . the others?"

She pointed off into the shadows under the trees. "They came . . . the riders from the valley . . . without warning."

Jess held her at arm's length, looking into her tearstained face. "Thank God you're all right," he said, and turned as Bob Rich came into the firelight behind him.

He had aged. There was blood caked on his cheek from a bullet cut on his head, above his right eye. His face seemed frozen into a cold, grim mask. He stopped a moment and crouched by the fire and warmed his hands.

"Hollister," he said. His voice was toneless. "Had about eight, nine riders with him. They left the sheep alone this time . . . just hit the camp. They . . . were looking for Dave."

Jess said, "Where're the others?"

"Back there," Bob said, inclining his head toward the trees, "with Hank!"

"Hank?"

Bob Rich took his time before replying. "Hank died a few minutes ago, Jess."

Jess left Luisa and followed Bob. Randy went with them. Larry and Chuck were crouched beside the body, laid out on a blanket. Below them the stream made its rushing tumbling sound.

They didn't say anything as Jess bent down and touched Hank Larrabee's face. There was a pain in him, dark and wild. Of all the men with him here, Hank had been closest to him: sharp-tongued, caustic, more than a ranch cook, closer to being a father.

The cold wind ran through the trees above. Slowly, Jess straightened.

Luisa came up to stand a few feet from him. The others looked at her but said nothing.

Jess said, "Where's Dave?"

She lifted a hand toward the pass. "He's not my husband," she said.

"Randy told me." Jess looked off into the darkness. "Why did he lie, Luisa?"

She shook her head sadly. "I don't know. I

guess he . . . he was ashamed of us. Of me. Of Urquillo. He is Dave's father, not a hired hand . . . my father, too."

Randy said harshly, "So he lied about that, too?"

Luisa nodded slowly.

"My father is a Basque, my mother was Mexican. But my brother and I were born in Texas." She was silent for a moment, looking back into another time, another place. "My brother was a sensitive boy. It was hard for him, when he grew up, to find that he was considered by some to be a second-class citizen. And being the son of a Basque sheepman didn't help."

The men were silent around Hank's body. A wind stirred a strand of gray hair on Hank's head. Luisa's gaze ranged over these men, stopping full on Jess.

"Does it matter to you, Jess?"

The big Texan shook his head. "It never did."

He looked at Randy standing beside Bob Rich, and the redheaded *segundo* shrugged. "Hell, I never cared for sheep. Habit, I guess. But what a man was or where his folks came from never bothered me."

He looked closely at Luisa now, frowning. "I was beginning to like Dave. I'm not sure now. And it's not because he's Mex, or a sheepherder, either."

It seemed to be the sentiment of the others.

Jess said quietly, "We'll bury Hank here, at the first light."

Luisa said, "You've done all you could . . . all of you . . ." Her voice was soft and sad. "My father and I . . . we didn't want this."

Jess said, "None of us did, Luisa," and turned as Maria came out of the darkness behind them.

The sheep dog whined softly and rubbed her muzzle against Jess' legs. She knew she was among friends. Then she went to Hank's body, and looked down into the still face and after a moment lay down beside him.

Luisa said, "You'll be leaving us now, Jess?"

Jess shook his head. "No," he said grimly. "We started out to see you get settled in Paradise Valley and that's where we're going!"

He looked at Randy, then at the others. Larry, Chuck and Bob Rich nodded. Randy growled, "Hank wouldn't want it any other way, Jess."

Jess walked back with Luisa to the gutted wagon. He crouched beside the old sheepman, his voice gentle. "How are you, Urquillo?"

The old man nodded, his eyes on Jess' face.

"We're taking you home," Jess said. "To the ranch you bought . . . in Paradise Valley."

Urquillo's eyes flickered. "You . . .will help?"

"We're in this together," Jess said. "All the way."

Standing behind him, Luisa's eyes filled with tears. She turned away as Jess straightened, not wanting him to see her cry again.

They buried Hank on the riverbank, in the cold light of dawn. At the head of the grave they erected a small cross. They carved no name or epitaph on it; for those who didn't know Hank it wouldn't matter. For the men standing silent, with bowed heads, the memory would never die.

Dave came walking in as they were hitching the team to the gutted wagon: footsore, weary, leading a limping horse. He paused to survey the scene, his face grim. Luisa was standing by her father. He let his horse drift as he went to them.

"Thank God," he said, "you're all right."

Jess moved toward him, bulking big and solid against the paling sky. The others waited.

Jess said, "Where've you been?"

Dave looked at him, eyes narrow, cold. "Making a deal," he said. His voice was defiant. "You can go home now . . . all of you."

"No," Jess said grimly. "Not all of us, Dave, Hank will be staying here . . . for good."

Dave stiffened. "I'm sorry," he said. Then: "Hollister?"

Jess nodded.

"So I heard," Dave muttered. "I tried to get back before. . . ." He shrugged. "I walked a hell of a long way, Jess."

"Heard?" Jess' gaze lay hard on Dave's face. "Where did you hear?"

"Doesn't matter," Dave said roughly. He turned to Luisa. "No more trouble," he said. "We're turning back. We'll find some other place."

Urquillo was leaning heavily against the wagon; he turned slowly to face his son.

"No," he said thickly. "We go home."

Dave said, "Tell him, Luisa. He doesn't understand. I made a deal with John Hendrix." He turned and eyed Jess, the men behind him. "Fifteen thousand dollars," he said, his eyes cold and challenging. "That's what he and the other cattlemen are paying me to turn back to stay out of Paradise Valley!"

"What are they paying for Hank?" Jess asked softly.

Dave licked his lips. "Not my fault," he said. Then, hard and uncaring: "Texan against Texan . . . doesn't concern me."

"Doesn't it?" Jess' voice was grim. "You're a Texan, too!"

Dave glanced at his sister.

"She told us," Jess said. Then, harsh: "You got us here on a lie, Dave. But you're not selling out now. Not us . . . not your sister . . . not your father."

Dave backed off slowly, his hand drifting toward his holstered gun.

"I made them pay," he said bitterly. "That's all I wanted." His gaze locked on Jess. "Why should you care now?"

"You don't know me very well, do you?" Jess said quietly. "When I start something I see it through!"

Dave licked his lips. "I made a deal with Hendrix."

"You made a deal with us," Jess said, and his voice held a wicked note in it now. "With us —

and with Hank back there."

"No!" Dave stopped now, his fingers on his gun, "I planned it . . . a long time. You're not stopping me, Jess . . . not now."

His hand came up quickly with a gun. "Not now." He turned slightly as Urquillo pushed away from the wagon and came toward him. The old man walked slowly, holding himself erect with an effort. He came up to Dave and slapped his face, jerking his head around.

"Pa!" Dave choked. "Pa . . . it's for you, too."

He staggered as the old man slapped him again; slowly he lowered his Colt.

Urquillo made a gesture toward Jess and the men behind him. "They are our friends," he said. "We do not quarrel with friends."

Dave brushed a hand across his mouth. "Pa . . ."

"We go home," Urquillo said. "To the fine ranch you bought for us."

Slowly Dave's gaze went from his father, to Luisa, to Jess and the men ranged behind him.

"You had a raw deal, back in Texas," Jess said. "We'll see you get a better one in Paradise Valley!"

They helped Urquillo up to the seat beside Luisa. The girl drove, leaving the charred chest behind. There was nothing there she could salvage.

Randy remained behind, with Larry, Chuck and Bob Rich. He had protested angrily, but Jess had overruled him. Luisa was driving the wagon; Randy and the others would drive the sheep.

They were going into Paradise Valley, come hell or high water!

Jess and Dave rode on ahead: a sheepman and a Texas trail boss with a cold and bitter wind howling in their faces.

XIX

John Hendrix stepped out onto his broad veranda, his foreman, Jedman, by his side. He faced the two riders in the yard with a cold wind whipping chimney smoke into a flat gray banner away from the house.

A half-dozen of his men were ranged behind Jess and Dave, watchful and ready.

The white-haired rancher's gaze held hard on Dave's face.

"You came too early," he said shortly. "I talked to Ned Sparrow and Lou Bretman last night.

"The deal's off!" Dave said. His voice was flat, but without anger.

Hendrix eyed him for a moment, then shifted his attention to Jess.

"Your doing?"

Jess shrugged. "We're coming up the pass," he said. "I wanted you to know."

Hendrix's face was still. "You'll have trouble."

"We already did," Jess said grimly. "That's why I'm here!"

He leaned forward in saddle, his eyes hard and unrelenting on the old rancher. "I always considered you a fair man, John. But there's one thing I have to know." He let his gaze drift over the men behind him before coming back to Hendrick.

"Any of your men in the bunch that raided the sheep camp last night?"

Hendrix frowned. "No," he said. He looked at his foreman. Jedman shook his head.

Jess said, "Hollister had eight or nine men with him. I'm glad none of them were yours, John."

Hendrix said, "Wait," as Jess started to swing away. "If Hollister raided your camp last night I didn't know it. I don't think Lou did, either. Or Ned Sparrow."

"That's what I'm going to find out," Jess said grimly. He paused, his hard gaze judging the rancher.

"You been losing cows, John?"

Jedman growled, "How'd you know, Jess?"

Jess looked at Dave.

"I ran into the sheriff," Dave said, "last night after I left here. I trailed him to my place . . . the Jenkins ranch. He met someone there he called Red." Dave shrugged. "They talked about moving rebranded cows south, out of the badlands hideout."

Hendrix frowned. "You sure?"

134

Jess said, "Why don't you find out, John?"

The rancher turned to his foreman. "Take all the men you need . . . check it out." He turned to Jess. "Wait for me. I'm riding with you to Lou Bretman's place!"

Lou Bretman was coming out of his barn when they rode up. A couple of his men came out of the bunkhouse to watch.

He eyed Jess sourly. "Heard you broke jail last night. Come for your cut, you damned traitor?"

John said, "Hold it, Lou. The deal's off."

Lou eyed them with open hostility. "Then what are you here for?"

"Hollister," Jess said. "Where is he?"

Lou said, "Rode into town." Then, harsh and angry: "Get out of here!"

Hendrick leaned over his saddlehorn. "Lou," he said quietly, "Hollister rode down to that sheep camp last night. Burned the wagon, killed one of Jess' men. Did you send him?"

Bretman stiffened. "No," he said. "I didn't send him the first time, either. But you know how I feel about sheep, John."

"Yeah," Hendrix cut in, "maybe that's the trouble, Lou. We've been so blinded by the thought of a sheepman settling in the valley we've been letting rustlers have a free hand with our stock."

Bretman said, "What are you talking about, John?"

"Hollister and Tennelly," John said. "Work-

135

ing with a bunch of rustlers out of the badlands. They been using the Jenkins place . . . that's why they didn't want Dave Owens here."

Bretman shook his head. "When'd you find that out, John?"

"I didn't," Hendrix answered. "Dave did. But I knew I was losing stock for some time. And old Jenkins hinted at it, but I didn't pay much attention to him, and he was an irascible sort, anyway. So he just shut up and sold out."

Bretman looked at Dave. "Maybe he's lying," he said to Hendrix.

The white-haired rancher nodded. "Maybe. Why don't you find out? Send some men, like I did, out past the Jenkins' place."

Jess was swinging away. "Do that," he said coldly. "But I want Hollister."

"And Tennelly," Dave said. There was a bitter smile in his eyes as he whirled and rode after Jess Riley.

Hendrix cut in front of Bretman as he started for the house.

"Lou — we better ride over and have a long hard talk with Ned Sparrow."

Bretman paused, looking up at the hard-faced rancher. "Hollister," he said and he was talking to himself. Then he nodded. "Be right with you, John."

Clay Hollister was in the Cimmaron Bar, nervously holding a drink and waiting for Tennelly. The sheriff had not come back from his meeting with Red and he knew that Jess Riley was loose somewhere, along with Dave Owens. And Jess would not be forgetting the raid last night!

He glanced at the wall clock and cursed softly. He'd wait a little longer, then he'd be riding on.

He had not figured on things going wrong. He had found out only after he had returned that Lou Bretman and Ned Sparrow had agreed to pay Owens off. But the damage had already been done.

He finished his drink and glanced at the clock again and Cimmaron, drifting over, said, "You look ragged, Clay. Bretman been working you too hard?"

Hollister ignored him. He poured himself another drink and then, hearing a rider on the street outside, he turned, thinking: *Damn you, Tennelly . . . it's about time.*

He went quickly to the door, leaving his drink. He pushed aside the batwings and stepped out on the walk, his gaze turning to the rider in the street. Jess said sharply, "Clay — I've come looking for you!"

Hollister froze. He saw Dave Owens up the street, behind Jess; he was mounted, waiting, and in that moment Clay Hollister knew he had waited too long.

"Jess," he said. "I . . . I only wanted to scare them off. I . . ."

Jess said, "You're a liar, Clay!" and there was a finality in his voice that drove Clay's hand down to his gun. He got off one wild shot before Riley's bullets drove him back into the batwings.

Jess dismounted and walked to Hollister lying half inside the saloon. Cimmaron was behind his bar, staring. The few people at the tables did not move.

The Texas trail boss hunkered down over Hollister. "Where's Tennelly?"

Hollister's eyes were wide, staring; a thin trickle of blood seeped from a corner of his mouth.

"Coming back . . . soon . . ." he sighed and then his head rolled and the life went out of him.

Jess turned to Dave riding up. "We'll wait," he said, and Dave nodded grimly.

Cal Tennelly rode into Bentley a half-hour later: a tall, rangy man with a streak of cruelness few people saw. He was unaware of what had happened, but caution crept into him as he sensed a quiet in the town — a stillness at odds with the hour of the day.

The main street was all but deserted. The few people he saw moved quickly indoors.

The sheriff had circled back from the badlands, coming in from the south now, along the road to Pine Bluffs, and he had missed seeing Hendrix's riders.

His gaze went to the Cimmaron Bar; Hollister was probably waiting for him inside. But he decided to ride on to the law office first, like a man just back from a long trip on official business.

He pulled up at the rail and dismounted and

the door opened as he turned.

Dave said, "I've been waiting a long time, sheriff!"

Tennelly stood very still, a thousand thoughts whirling through his head.

"Hollister's dead," Dave said easily. "Case you're wondering. Jess Riley killed him."

Tennelly still didn't move.

"There's thirty men riding into the badlands," Dave went on. "I don't think Red and his men will get away."

A small sigh gusted from the sheriff. "Hollister talk?"

Dave said evenly, "You've got a choice, sheriff. A hanging — or. . . ." He let his hand hang over his Colt butt. "I'm calling you, Tennelly," and his voice rode hard now, deep and bitter: "Me, a sheepman."

Tennelly drew and shot and shot once more as he was falling back against his horse. His eyes clouded and he tried to fire once more, but his fingers suddenly wouldn't respond and his gun slid out of his hand. He eyed it for a moment, his vision dimming, before he fell.

Jess Riley moved up behind Dave. The sheepman was leaning against the doorframe, his left arm limp. Blood dropped from his fingertips to the scarred, wooden step below.

Jess said quietly, "We'll get that arm bandaged, Dave. Then we'll go home."

Jess Riley said good-bye to Luisa on the steps

139

of the Jenkins place. Dave and Urquillo watched, smiling. Bob Rich, Larry and Chuck were mounted, waiting.

The sheep were grazing, scattered along the ridges. Jess knew there would be no more trouble: not with the cattlemen in Paradise Valley.

Some of them, like Ned Sparrow and Lou Bretman, didn't like it. But in time they would learn to get along.

For Jess Riley was coming back.

He promised Luisa that — as soon as he settled his affairs in Texas. He kissed her in front of the men, then mounted and rode away with his companions falling in behind him.

But Luisa knew he would return. For Jess Riley was a man of his word.

The employees of G.K. Hall hope you have enjoyed this Large Print book. All our Large Print titles are designed for easy reading, and all our books are made to last. Other G.K. Hall books are available at your library, through selected bookstores, or directly from us.

For information about titles, please call:

(800) 257-5157

To share your comments, please write:

Publisher
G.K. Hall & Co.
P.O. Box 159
Thorndike, ME 04986